MISSOURI MAMA

Edwards was within twenty yards. McCoy wanted to gun the man down with four shots to the heart the way Edwards had the last bank president, but McCoy was a lawman and had to call out for Edwards to surrender first.

His instructions had been to bring Edwards back alive. They wanted a show trial in Boise to prove that it was a tough town on bank robbers. He'd do his damnedest.

Then McCoy could see the dripping beard of the outlaw, the familiar face, the black eyes and too large nose and even the sneer.

McCoy took out his six-gun and laid it beside the rock. It was time.

"You're under arrest, Edwards," Spur bellowed. "Don't move or you're a dead man!"

SPUR #37

MISSOURI MAMA

DIRK FLETCHER

LEISURE BOOKS NEW YORK CITY

A LEISURE BOOK®

June 2006

Published by

Dorchester Publishing Co., Inc.
200 Madison Avenue
New York, NY 10016

ISBN 0-8439-3341-0

Printed in the United States of America.

Visit us on the web at www.dorchesterpub.com.

MISSOURI MAMA

Chapter One

United States Secret Service Agent Spur McCoy didn't feel the rain anymore. He was soaked to his long johns, his boots were a soggy bog, and his hat had fallen off so many times in the scramble through this damned brush in the wilds of Idaho that his hair was wet as well.

He lay now in a small ravine watching the slow movements of his target below. Blade Edwards had slipped through the net thrown around him for five years, but now McCoy was going to grab the slippery son of a bitch. He had been wanted for bank robbery for more than six years. At the last bank he had killed three people and laughed about it as he fled.

If at all possible, McCoy wanted this to be the end of the trail for Edwards who bragged that he would never be taken alive. McCoy wondered what tricks he had up his soggy sleeve this time.

Edwards kept moving upward. He had no idea that McCoy had surged past him in the last thunderstorm. Lightning had smashed down a dozen of the tall fir trees, and the usually even-tempered Idaho drizzle turned into a downpour that made rushing streams in even the smallest gullies.

McCoy had holstered his Peacemaker .45, slung his Spencer repeating rifle over his shoulder and charged up this lonesome Idaho hillside through the heart of the cloudburst to get in front of the fugitive and have a place of his own choosing for the final showdown.

It had worked, since Edwards evidently had taken some protection during the downpour. Spur had chosen his spot carefully. He knew that Edwards was on foot and working hard up the slopes to get over Snowfall Pass and to the tiny town of Snowfall on the other side. For years it had been a gathering point for drifters and men on the run from every crime in the book. They tolerated one another and permitted no law whatsoever in the vicinity. It served as a safe haven for from 15 to 50 outlaws, depending on the time of year and the heat of the chase.

McCoy lay in his chosen spot and watched the fugitive working his way slowly up the narrow valley. It was little more than a canyon, and a rushing stream ten feet wide still boiled down the center of it.

Edwards kept just to the side of the water where the ground was the most level and trudged upward. He had a rifle slung over his shoulder muzzle down and a six-gun holstered on his left hip. The government man would make no mistakes this time. He had let Edwards get away once two years ago due to a gun

Edwards had hidden in his crotch. Never again.

McCoy had picked a spot where two boulders sat with a crevice about a foot wide between them. It was a made-to-order firing slot. He had bent down a foot-high young fir in front of the rocks, and he had a perfect field of fire.

His spot was less than 50 feet from the edge of the stream, and Edwards was now trudging uphill on this side of the water.

McCoy felt more water dripping through his slicker, his leather jacket, his shirt and long johns. He brushed wetness off his eyebrows and checked on Blade Edwards through the continuing soft rainfall.

The killer kept coming, head down, sure of himself now. He must have figured that last shootout at the base of the mountain had put down McCoy who had cried out in pain once, but Edwards had not investigated to see if he had wounded or killed the government agent.

Now things would be different. There was absolutely no cover except the water itself in the small gully. At this point it narrowed to 100 feet across, and the water wouldn't be deep enough to cover an ankle-high boot.

McCoy shifted the Spencer slightly to track the fugitive. Edwards was 50 yards downhill working slowly upward. McCoy had sighted in this weapon three days ago. It fired a shade high and to the right at 100 yards. At 50 feet there would be little drift. He made sure the safety was off and checked the breech. One round was loaded, and seven more of the .52 caliber stingers were in the tube through the stock. He could fire eight times, as fast as he could work the lever under the trigger.

Now Edwards was within 20 yards. McCoy wanted to gun the man down with four shots to the heart the way Edwards had the last bank president, but McCoy was a lawman and had to call out for Edwards to surrender first. The killer wouldn't give up. So Spur's first shot would be in the shoulder while he was fairly stationary. Hopefully he could put Edwards down right away.

McCoy's instructions had been to bring the man back alive. They wanted a show trial in Boise to prove that it was a tough town on bank robbers. He'd do his damnedest.

Ten yards.

Then McCoy could see the dripping beard of the outlaw, the familiar face, the black eyes and too large nose and even the sneer coming through the beard.

McCoy took out his six-gun and laid it beside the rock. It was time.

"You're under arrest, Edwards," Spur bellowed. "Don't move or you're a dead man."

Even before he got out the third word, the killer made his play. He whipped up the rifle and triggered a shot at the rocks as he dove down the slope.

McCoy tracked him and fired, just as Edwards's slug chipped stone off the inside of the rock a foot over McCoy's head. The agent levered another round in as the killer rolled and fired. This time he saw the bullet hit Edwards in the left shoulder. Edwards kept rolling. McCoy lifted to fire again when another round from the fugitive chipped more shards inside the right boulder, spraying his cheek with sharp splinters of rock.

McCoy wiped blood off his cheek and dropped lower, firing a third time. This one caught Edwards just as he surged to his feet. It took him in the right shoulder and jolted the rifle from his hand.

The big .52 caliber bullet at such close range slammed Edwards to the ground where he lay panting, the fine rain still falling, diluting the blood that showed on his shoulder even through his clothes.

"Give it up, Edwards. You're outgunned this time. Take your chances with a jury."

"Got more of a chance with you, McCoy. Thought I had you that last go-round. You faked that hit, right?"

"Throw out your six-gun and your hidden weapons, Edwards, then we'll talk."

"Got nothing hidden."

"Sure, and a goose doesn't have feathers. All I have to do is deliver you alive. I can put a slug into your right kneecap. You want to walk back down the mountain hopping all the way?"

Slowly Edwards tossed his six-gun up the slope.

"Easy now. Sit up if you have to, but I want to see at least two derringers," McCoy barked.

Edwards eased upward so he sat in the slowly falling rain. Water dripped off the slouch brown hat. His eyes glared at McCoy's position, then he slid a derringer from his jacket pocket under the slicker.

"That's all I got," Edwards called.

"Like hell. You always carry two, sometimes three. Get another one out or that kneecap goes."

"Damnit, McCoy, you know me too well. In my crotch. Take me a minute."

McCoy kept the Spencer trained on the man as he fumbled with his clothes. A moment later a derringer slid out of his hand and landed six feet away. It would have done him no good to fire either of them at this range.

"Now, stand up and walk this way. When you get within twenty feet of the rocks, I want you to turn around and put both hands behind you."

"Damn you, McCoy. You don't give a man a chance."

"That's the whole idea, Edwards. The same way you shot down those three in that last bank job."

"They talked back to me."

"You're talking back to me, Edwards. Now get over here and we both can get out of this rain."

Edwards moved slowly, shuffling toward McCoy. When he was there he stopped.

"This close enough?"

"Yeah, turn around."

McCoy had the Spencer trained on the man's left shoulder. This would be the time if Edwards was going to try anything else. The robber seemed to sigh, then he flexed both arm and started to put them behind him. When moved his left arm again, a derringer slid into his hand from his sleeve, and the two weapons went off almost at the same time.

Edward's half-aimed slug from the derringer tore through McCoy's slicker, his jacket's left sleeve and shirt before it sliced a groove in his left shoulder. It burned like hell.

McCoy's own round had found its mark on the gunman's left shoulder, spinning him backward ten feet down the slope. McCoy saw the derringer fly out of Edward's hand, and the secret agent came from behind the boulders and charged forward.

Edwards lay on his back screaming. McCoy planted one soggy boot in the middle of his back, pulled hand-cuffs from his belt and quickly cuffed the man's hands behind him.

"Edwards, it's the end of the game for you. The only thing you have to look forward to now is a nice dry jail cell and a hangman's noose. At least you have to walk back to the horses. That's the only reason I didn't shoot you in the leg."

It took McCoy the rest of the day to get back to the small town of Riley, Idaho. The sheriff took charge of Edwards for the night, and two days later McCoy turned Edwards over to the federal court in Boise, Idaho.

He wired his office in St. Louis and got back a curt reply that he had no messages waiting from him from General Halleck, the number two man in the United Secret Service and his boss in Washington.

McCoy grinned. For the first time in six months he had a chance to get back to his office in St. Louis and sleep in his own bed again. It didn't happen often. He wondered if Lucinda would still be there.

Chapter Two

Agent Spur McCoy's office in St. Louis, Missouri, consisted of space leased by the government on a yearly basis in the venerable Claymore Hotel. It was really two rooms—one to live in and a second, smaller room where he could receive mail, have a desk and represent Capital Investigations of Washington D.C., the cover name for the United States Secret Service.

McCoy had wired ahead, and when he arrived in the office Thursday morning, he found it open, the room aired out, and the mail neatly sorted and stacked. Behind this miracle of work stood Priscilla Quincy, a small lady of 24 with short red hair, a winsome smile and a neat and trim little figure. She smiled and nodded.

"Good morning, Agent McCoy."

"You're the best helper in the world, Quincy. I see you have things in good shape. First, any work orders from the general?"

"For once, Mr. McCoy, not a single one. Isn't that great? You can have some time to repair your weapons, buy new clothes and have a small rest between assignments for a change."

Her glorious smile was worth the long train ride. "The rest of the mail?"

"I put it into three piles: throw away, read only if interested, and two scented envelopes mailed from right here in St. Louis."

"Two scented letters . . . well, yes, I'll take those. Why don't I see to the rest of my mail after my bath and some clean clothes? I just got off the Limited from Omaha and points west."

"Mr. McCoy?"

He had just opened the connecting door into his room and now turned and nodded. "Yes?"

"It's good to have you back. You do look a little thin. I've got a great roast beef dinner I can have ready for you about six . . . if you're interested."

"Six. Let's see—it's ten-thirty now. Six might be fine. Can I let you know for sure a little later?"

Her excitement vaporized, and a hard glint came into her green eyes. "Yes, I see. For your information, Lucinda Ballenkamp is still in town, lives at the same house, runs the bank and is the prize catch of the century, relentlessly pursued by all the local bachelors."

McCoy grinned. "Thanks, Pris. Don't know what I'd do without you."

He vanished through the door and closed it. He'd arranged for hot water to be brought up since this hotel didn't have it piped in as yet to all of the rooms.

He stripped off his traveling clothes and then, naked, hurried back to the connecting door. He opened it a foot and pushed his head through.

"Oh, Pris, you better write out the usual telegram and take it down to the office and send it. Tell the general that I'm back and cleaning up my paper work here. That's all he needs to know. Thanks, Pris."

She stared at his head poking around the barely opened door, and her frown deepened. Pris opened her mouth to say something then closed it. He was about to shut the door when she held up her hand to stop him. She sat at the small desk where she was opening mail.

"Mr. McCoy, pardon me for asking, but are you stark naked?"

"Priscilla Quincy, what a perfectly outrageous thing for a proper young lady to be asking!" He couldn't hold his frown for long and grinned. "Right, Priscilla, about as naked as a newborn babe, but this is all of me you get to see or your pappy would use me for shotgun practice out on that big ranch of his."

Priscilla sighed. "Yes, you're right of course. That is, unless of course . . ."

"Pris, we've been over this before, remember? I'm not about to get myself hitched to you or any other young beautiful and wanton filly. So just be a good girl and open the mail and send that wire, so I can be officially here at my post awaiting the directions of our glorious leader."

Pris pouted for a moment, her red hair flouncing as she looked around quickly. Her eyes, almost as green as his, shot off a dozen sparks. "Of course, I could always tell the major that you overpowered me on the desk and had your way with me. Then he'd still use his shotgun, but it would be to get you to a church and a preacher."

McCoy nodded. "Good, we're back to that shotgun. You know you would never lie like that, Priscilla, and I know you would never make up a crazy story like that. So we can still be friends. Lovers are easy to find, little lady, but one good friend like you is worth a hundred lovers."

"That's what you told me six months ago the last time you were here."

"You remembered?"

"Of course. I just hope that one of these days you'll forget and open the door all the way."

"Not a chance," McCoy said with a big grin. "Now, pretty Pris, get your little bottom off that chair and send a wire to my boss. I've got hot water turning cold in here."

He closed the door firmly, threw the bolt and then stepped into the steaming water in the portable steel tub that was only half long enough for his legs.

Spur McCoy, ace agent for the United States Secret Service, had the whole western half of the country to cover until they got more men to help him. Then he'd first move his office to Denver, leave a man here and eventually move all the way to San Francisco, spotting agents along the way.

McCoy was big enough for the job. He stood six-two and weighed in at just over 185 pounds of hard muscles. He face was tanned and windburned from more time spent outdoors than in, and he usually wore a black, low-crowned, flat-topped Stetson with a wide flat brim and a row of Mexican silver coins around the headband.

He was suited to his job. He'd graduated from Harvard, spent enough time in the Civil War to come out an infantry captain and served a year in Washington D.C. as an aide to an old family friend who was a U.S. Senator from New York. When the Secret Service was formed, he rushed to join and had been with the service ever since. What he wanted now was three more agents in his area.

He stepped into the bath, got used to the near boiling water and settled down to soak. Then he opened the two scented letters and read them. Both were from Lucinda, written nearly a month apart. Both were almost the same, wishing he were back home so they could go out to the opera or to a concert.

Then there was the rest she wasn't saying. He looked over at his bed, which was freshly made each week whether he used it or not. It looked small, lumpy and uncomfortable. That nice big featherbed in Lucinda's master bedroom would be much better for his first night back in St. Louis.

Spur put the letters on the floor and soaked another five minutes before he began to wash himself.

He scrubbed away the days of train travel and even some Idaho grit and stepped from the tub clean and in need of a shave and a haircut. He gave himself a shave with some of the leftover hot water, then checked his pocket watch. 11:20 A.M.

He put on tweed town pants, a gray shirt, a black leather vest and a string tie. He pulled on his polished black, high topped cowboy boots and headed for the hall. He just had time to get to the St. Louis State Bank and invite Lucinda out to dinner—or did they call it lunch yet here in St. Louis?

He reached for the door to the hall when someone knocked on the connecting door to the office. He unlatched the bolt and opened the door.

Priscilla stood there with a big smile. "I sent the wire, and while I was there one came through for you." She handed him the envelope.

"Not an assignment already?"

"We won't know until we open the envelope, will we, Mr. McCoy?"

He tore open the end of the yellow and black envelope and read the wire:

"TO: SPUR MCCOY, CAPITAL INVESTIGATIONS, CLAYMORE HOTEL, ST. LOUIS. MO. NOTIFY ME OF YOUR ARRIVAL. AM SENDING TODAY, WEDNESDAY, 26 OCTOBER, A NEW AGENT FOR YOU TO WORK WITH ON YOUR NEXT ASSIGNMENT. TAKE TWO OR THREE DAYS TO GET TO KNOW EACH OTHER, DECIDE HOW YOU CAN BEST WORK TOGETHER. YOUR NEW ASSIGNMENT NOW BEING PUT TOGETHER. IT'S UNUSUAL. TAKE CARE OF THAT ARM WOUND. (YOU USUALLY HAVE BEEN SHOT SOMEWHERE.) DETAILS OF NEXT ASSIGNMENT COMING SPECIAL RAIL EXPRESS WITH HAND DELIVERY. SENDING: W. D. HALLECK, LT. GENERAL, US ARMY, CAPITAL INVESTIGATIONS, WASHINGTON D.C."

McCoy groaned and handed the telegram to Priscilla. "Take care of this. If the new agent comes while I'm out, show him some of our files. Try to figure out if he's a political appointee or if he's had any training. I'm going to go out to lunch."

"With Lucinda?"

"Hopefully." He turned and hurried out of the office before she could give him any more bad news. He worked alone, damnit! General Halleck knew that. Why was he sending out a second agent? Nothing said about him being permanent at least, just somebody to help him on this next assignment. Damn!

The St. Louis State Bank looked the same as it had six months ago. Solid blocks of granite had been carefully placed together into a two-story building that should stand for 200 years. He pushed through the heavy swinging door and stepped into the bank.

Five iron teller's cages were in a long counter, leaving a sizeable lobby. To the left were two closed doors and a desk with a woman sitting behind it.

When he stopped in front of her, she looked up and grinned.

"Yes, sir, and what can I do for you today?"

"I'm here to see Miss Ballenkamp in response to her letter."

"Who shall I say is calling?"

"Spur McCoy."

The woman's face fell, and she sighed. "Might have known," she mumbled as she rose and went to the first door marked "President". She knocked, then opened the door and said something. A moment later a tall blonde woman in a severely cut woman's suit rushed past her surprised secretary.

"Spur, I hoped you'd be back soon." She almost jumped into his arms, looked around the bank a moment, touched her hair and beamed, then motioned him into her office. "We better talk this over in my office, Mr. McCoy. Right this way."

The office door closed softly, and Lucinda Ballenkamp slid the bolt into its slot, making no sound. She turned and caught Spur's head and kissed him deeply, pushing hard against him and tightening her arms around his back like bands of shrinking rawhide.

When the kiss ended she sighed and leaned against his chest.

"You finally came back. It's been six months."

"About right. Looks like you're still running the bank. I hear you're fighting off the bachelors and fortune hunters."

"Yes, yes, yes—because I'm waiting for you, silly man." She kissed him again, then led him to a small couch at the side of the room.

"It's new. I sometimes have small catnaps in the afternoons. It peps me up."

"Ever have a catnap in the morning?"

"Not so close to the noon hour. I always take two hours off for what we're calling lunch now. That would seem like a better time for us to have that small nap."

"We'll lunch at your big house on the hill or your downtown apartment?" McCoy asked.

Lucinda was all a man could ask for. She was tall enough for McCoy at five-six and had long, honey-blonde hair that now fell nearly to her waist. She hadn't cut it in over a year.

Her cheekbones were high, making little round mounds when she smiled. Soft brown eyes showed under thick eyelashes.

Lucinda's face was a marvel of engineering and construction with a nose just right over a wide mouth that had nearly perfect white teeth. The top of the suit coat strained, holding in her full breasts. The pinched-in suit coat showed her figure to the best possible extent, even though the skirt of the suit hugged her hips and plunged within an inch of the floor. It was considered a business suit so it didn't have to touch the floor.

"Hey, Spur, I answered your question, but you didn't seem to have heard me."

"I was just undressing you with my eyes. When I do that with lots of enthusiasm, sometimes my ears don't work so well."

"Let's go to the apartment. It's closer and we'll have more time. In fact, it's a quarter to twelve, so let's leave right now. Yes, I want to be seen leaving with you. Maybe it'll put some pressure on you to stay at home and take care of my needs and put that little band of gold around my finger."

He kissed her hard, and she hung in his arms, eyes wide.

"Oh, God!" she breathed. "Let me get myself collected so it won't look like you made love to me on the couch, and we can get out of here."

Ten minutes later they were in a three-story apartment building which had an elevator with a steel cage.

"This thing really work?" McCoy asked.

"So far," she said, closing the door and pushing the buzzer twice. "Somebody down in the basement does something, and we go up to the third floor."

In her apartment, they went directly to the bedroom.

"Do you know how long it's been since—"

He kissed her, stopping the words, but she pulled away. "Damnit, McCoy, I'm saving myself for you. I haven't been with a man since I was with you last. I need you!"

She tore off the jacket of the suit, pulled up her white blouse under it and unbuttoned it, then pushed back her chemise so he could find her breasts.

He grinned, kissed her lips gently, then bent and kissed her surging breasts, working around one slowly until he came to the delicate pinkness of areola, then higher and higher until he licked her surging nipple. He kissed it, then bit it gently and a moment later moved to her other breast to repeat the ministrations.

"Oh, God, but that gets me moving. I want you deep inside me right now!"

She pulled up her skirt, pushed down her pink silk bloomers, kicked them off her feet, then dropped on the bed and opened her arms.

"If you take off your pants or do anything but open your fly, I'm gonna hit you in the face, Spur McCoy. Right now, dig him out and poke me about a hundred times. I'm on fire! I'm so hot I don't think I can stand it another minute without you inside my little hole!"

McCoy did as he was instructed. His fly buttons rubbed her tender flesh, but she didn't seem to notice.

"Hot and fast and hard, like you've been waiting for

me all these months, too. Now, McCoy, fuck me hard right now."

McCoy had been needing her ever since he saw her in the bank, and now he plunged into the glory of her pink slot and found they still fitted together perfectly. He drove in with long hard strokes, stimulating as much of her tender parts as he could each time.

On the fourth stroke she shivered and then wailed, and a long series of vibrations were followed at once by sharp jolting spasms that shook her to her very core.

It was two or three minutes before Lucinda's climax abated and she openned her eyes.

"Oh, God, what a good one!" Then she began humping against him. It was her signal that it was his turn, and he blasted into her hard again and soon sensed the gushing starting high up in his groin and rushing forward.

He poked harder and harder, and just as he was about to fcel he had to stop to breathe, he came in a series of six jolts that he thought would put an end to the entire world.

McCoy grunted and brayed as he climaxed, then his panting became softer and softer until it gave way to his near normal breathing.

"Oh, God, I don't see how anything could ever be better—or even as good. Not with anyone else, I assure you. Yes, I've had men before you, smarty pants, but not one of them ever measured up to you." She laughed. "In fact I don't think any two of them put together ever measured up to your performance. Marvelous."

She turned her head, closed her eyes and went to sleep. This simple little action always surprised him. Somehow, what put other women on edge for a half hour acted upon Lucinda as a sleeping potion.

He knew if he moved he'd awaken her. He rested on the softness of her body, still enclosed by her and still thinking of her. A moment later he shut his eyes and dozed off. He'd never done that before. He came back to consciousness with a start and saw that she was awake and watching him.

"I was so good that it put you to sleep?"

"Better than that. You knocked me unconscious." He pulled away from her, and they both sat up on the side of the bed.

"I hope you weren't hungry. I didn't even think about having some lunch sent up."

"We can eat anytime."

"Time . . . what time is it? I have an important conference at two-thirty with some builders. I want to do the financing on a big new building they want to put up. Ten stories high almost and downtown. They haven't even suggested how much money they will need, but I want to finance it. I'll have to sell some of my other investments, but this is exactly why Daddy built up the bank—so we could help local people get ahead."

"And for the usual seven percent."

She threw an angry glance at him. "We haven't talked about the loan rate either. It could be less than that for this much money and over a ten year payback."

They stopped talking business then. It was early, and they had plenty of time. They sat near the window and looked out on St. Louis and the country beyond.

"It's a growing, wonderful town," Lucinda said. "I want to be a big part of that growth. That's why we can't spend all afternoon here in bed."

Twice more they made love, then she arrived back at the bank with ten minutes to spare.

McCoy checked in with his office, but Priscilla said no one had come and that there was nothing interesting in the mail, unless he wanted to buy some land in Arizona.

He went about his business of gathering up his affairs. There were some reports Priscilla gave him that he needed to read, initial and send back to Washington. She showed him two more interesting letters from people who knew of some gigantic fraud against the government. He had no idea how they got his name and address.

Later he went out and bought a new carpetbag, one that he could collapse and tie behind a saddle if need be or could stack full of clothes and goods and stow it on the train. He needed some new clothes and picked out two pair of town pants, two pair of jeans, a hard-wearing blue shirt for range wear and a pair of dress shirts. Then he had his hat cleaned and blocked.

He also had his Peacemaker given an overhaul by Bernard, his favorite gunsmith. He checked his backup Peacemaker, remembered that it had never been fired and took it down to Bernard's test range to be sure it was somewhat accurate.

"Low and right an inch at thirty feet," Bernard determined. "Be sure which weapon you have. Your number one Peacemaker fires high and to the right, the other one low and to the right. Could make a difference."

Spur had never carried a hidden gun, but now he bought one—a neat little derringer taking the same .45 rounds that fit his Peacemaker. When he got back to the office, he was satisfied. He had done most of the things he needed to do, had put Lucinda's charms to the test, had a dinner date with her for tonight after the bank closed, and all was right with the world.

It was after four in the afternoon when he breezed into his office and stopped short.

A woman sat in a chair next to the desk and was seemingly in an animated conversation with Priscilla. When he came in both stood up as if they were in a conspiracy against him.

The other woman was about five-five with jet black hair, cut short with bangs across the forehead and shaped tightly against her head in back. She wore a traveling dress that couldn't hide her big breasts but did dip in delightfully at the waist before it flared over her hips and hit the floor.

McCoy saw flashes of blue eyes over a turned-up nose, small mouth and firm chin. She was a pretty woman, and he figured her at about 24.

Priscilla found her voice first. "Oh, Mr. McCoy, I'd like you to meet Jessica Flanders. That's Secret Service Agent Jessica Flanders. She's the new agent sent from Washington to help you on your next assignment."

Chapter Three

Spur McCoy leaned against the wall. Never in his life had he been more surprised, and that, mixed with indignation and outrage bordering on anger, forced him to turn toward the door as he fought to control himself.

When he looked back at the women, his face had gone stiff and cold. He held out his hand. "Welcome to St. Louis, Agent Flanders."

She shook his hand briefly, a firm quick pressure, then released it.

"Agent McCoy, I know that you're angry. Priscilla told me that the general didn't warn you that I was a woman. I'm sorry. I had no idea that you were so . . . so set in your ways." Her eyes hardened, and her firm chin lifted a notch.

"However, Agent McCoy, I, too, am an agent of the United States Secret Service, and I have been assigned here to work on an upcoming case. I'm not

sure what it is just yet, but I can guess that it has
something to do with forgery or the counterfeiting of
United States bank notes. I've spent the better part
of a year in our Washington office working on such
cases. Some people think that I'm an expert in the
field. The general must have sent me here to help
you on some upcoming forgery or counterfeiting case
because of my experience."

McCoy had dropped his hand to his side and now
nodded routinely.

"Yes, I understand your orders, Miss Flanders. We
all get orders, and we all have to follow them—myself
as well. If this new assignment is about counterfeiting,
I'm sure your expertise will be invaluable."

He turned to Priscilla. "Anything new yet on those
orders from the general?"

"Not a thing, Mr. McCoy."

"They'll come. Right now we'll need another desk in
here for Agent Flanders."

"I've taken care of that already, Mr. McCoy. The
hotel said that they'll have one up here before closing
time tonight. I've laid out some supplies that Agent
Flanders will need. I think all of that is well in hand."

McCoy nodded again as he tried hard not to show his
emotions. "Good, good. Anything I need to look at in
the mail?"

"No sir. We went over most of that before."

"Fine. I'll be checking out for today then. I'll be back
tomorrow about nine."

He went out the door with a nod to both women.
Agent Spur McCoy controlled himself until he was
through the hallway and halfway down the steps to the

first floor before he exploded. He slammed the flat of his hand against the wall twice, then hurried out the side door of the hotel into the alley where he let out a long and resounding, "No, damnit!"

McCoy took a deep breath and shook his head. Not only an associate agent, but a goddamned woman agent! Yes, he knew there were three or four now in the service, but he never figured that he'd even meet one, let alone have to work hand in glove with one.

"Damnit to hell!" McCoy growled as he walked out of the alley and down the street to the first saloon he came to—Raunchy Bill's Saloon.

Since it was the closest watering hole to the office, McCoy had been in it more than a few times. The first drink was always on the house from Raunchy Bill. He slammed through the swinging doors and pointed one finger at Willis the barkeep. The man promptly took a bottle of bourbon off the back shelf and poured a shot for McCoy, then stood there, not even corking the bottle, waiting for the first drink to vanish. It did.

"One more, Willis. I am not going to get stinking drunk, but I should. If I do, you know where I live?"

Willis nodded. He'd been through this routine with McCoy at least a dozen times, but he'd never had to pour the detective into his room at the Claymore Hotel. Willis had no idea McCoy worked for the government.

"Good. Now put the rest of that bottle on my tab and tell them painted whores to stay a half mile away from my table. Tonight I hate all women."

For an hour, McCoy sat and stared at the third shot of whiskey. All that time he was fighting with himself about whether he should refuse the assignment when it came and wire the general that he must either take the woman agent back or McCoy would resign.

"What I goddamn will not do is work a case with a goddamn woman agent," McCoy mumbled to himself. Once that was out in the open and at least spoken softly, McCoy felt a little bit mollified. He began to see small cracks of light in the total darkness, little slivers of brightness that helped illuminate his predicament.

Yes, he could do that. He would make her investigate every minutia of the case, send her on trips to Omaha and Cheyenne and Chicago to get evidence, send her on background checks on a suspect, run her pretty little ass off in first one direction and then another. When she was out of his hair, he would be able to work on the case without any interference from her and without having to protect her pretty little tits.

McCoy frowned. Yes, she did have good tits that fairly screamed to be let out. He shook his head. He was getting drunk. She was too tall. He liked short women. Today he liked short women. She was too skinny. He liked a woman with some meat on her bones so her pelvis didn't slam into his. Yeah, a little more meat on Agent Jessica Flanders' sleek and slender little ass would make her a much better roll in the hay.

He jammed the cork back in the bottle of bourbon, gave the third shot to the drunk at the next table and found himself a game of dime limit poker that already had four players. Five was just about right for good betting.

McCoy played until 2:00 A.M. In the course of the evening he had been as much as $25 ahead and $10 behind. He wound up the last hand winning on a bluff with his opener pair of jacks and crawled out of the saloon tired, no wiser, and two dollars richer.

The next morning McCoy awoke at 7:00. It had been years since he had slept in past 6:30 when he was alone in bed. He dressed, shaved, combed his longish dark hair and remembered he hadn't seen a barber yesterday as he had planned. He walked two blocks out of the way to a small café where he had a lumberjack's breakfast. He didn't want to run into Miss Pussyfoot Agent Flanders before he had to. It would be hard enough when he got to the office.

After breakfast he stopped at his usual barber who scolded him for not coming in more often for his haircut. McCoy liked his hair to hang long around his neck, just touching his collar and half-hiding his ears. No businessman's cut for him.

He arrived at the office at 8:30 and found both women already there. A new desk huddled in one corner of the room with Agent Flanders sitting behind it reading notices from the head office and recent mailings.

Her short, dark hair clung to her head like a helmet and not a strand was out of place. She looked up and smiled, then the look faded as she saw the grim expression on McCoy's face.

"Good, you're here, Flanders. What's your weapon?"

"My weapon? Oh, I have a five shot .38 caliber Smith and Wesson with a four-inch barrel. I carry it in my reticule, but I also have a gunbelt and side leather if the occasion demands it."

"Can you shoot?"

"Yes."

"Good. Let's go down to Bernard's range in back of his gunshop and see what you can do."

"Right now?"

"If you're going to back me up, I want to be sure you can use that little peashooter. Just a minute while I get my backup Peacemaker."

He barged into his room, brought back his spare .45 Colt and nodded at the door. He did not wait for her or open the door and let her go out first. McCoy marched out of the room, down the hall and let her catch up when she could.

She wore a proper dress, a matching colored sweater for the fall chill and a small hat that blended in with the color scheme. Just what every Secret Service agent should wear, he groused to himself.

Bernard wasn't open yet, so they went around to the alley directly behind his shop where the gunsmith had set up a shooting range. McCoy put five tin cans on the stack of railroad ties that Bernard had positioned to stop bullets. They fired from the alley into the barricade that was built two feet in back of the rear wall of the gunshop. That way nobody complained about stray rounds. The city told Bernard he would have to move his testing range out of the downtown area, but nobody followed up on it. That had been two years ago.

McCoy marked off a line in the dust 20 feet from the row of five cans sitting on the rail ties.

He turned to her. "Agent Flanders, you're walking down a street in a small Western town and one of the bad guys opens up on you with a handgun from thirty feet away. The bad guy is the second can on the right in that line. What will you do?"

The reticule over her shoulder flipped open, her left hand darted in and brought out the short-barreled .38. Her thumb had cocked the weapon before it cleared the reticule's side. She brought it up in a quick point and fired.

The second can from the right slammed backward off the rail tie. She fired four more times, and all five of the tin cans flew into the air.

"After that I'd duck down somewhere and reload," Agent Flanders said.

McCoy's mouth dropped open for just a moment, but long enough for her to see.

"Fine, so you can shoot. You better reload your piece now so it'll be ready in case you need it. How many rounds do you carry with you?"

"Forty. I used to carry twenty, but once I was in a shootout with four forgers and I ran dry. I promised myself never to be out of rounds again."

He watched her as she opened the cylinder, flipped out the spent brass, quickly loaded in five new rounds and closed the weapon with the hammer resting on the empty chamber.

"Put it away and try this one." He handed her his backup .45 Peacemaker, the one that fired an inch to the right and high. Then he went to the target and set up three more cans on the ties.

Back at the 20 foot line, he watched her hefting the Colt. McCoy sat down on the ground and asked her for the Colt which she handed over. He lay it beside his right hand in the alley and looked up.

"Your weapon is not available—lost, stolen, fouled. I get hit and can't fire. Those three cans up there are the bad guys ready to kill us both. What do you do? Now!"

Jessica Flanders dropped to one knee beside him, swept up his .45, held it with both hands and knocked down two of the three cans with three rounds.

McCoy stood and took the weapon from her. He replaced the three rounds and slowly nodded.

"Agent Flanders, looks like you can shoot. A damn good thing. That's what keeps agents alive out here in the West. How far west have you been?"

"Once to San Francisco, once to Denver. I didn't see much of the small town action."

"At least you're honest."

She turned and faced him with a concerned look on her countenance.

"Agent McCoy, I realize that you were stunned and angered when I reported in as your backup on this upcoming assignment. I'm sorry, but there's nothing I can do about my gender. Just let me do my job, that's all that I ask. Now if this petty little testing is over, let's get back to the office. We got a wire first thing this morning that our orders would be in on the

Railway Express which should arrive in our office a
little after nine"

"About now," McCoy said.

"Yes, about now."

When they got back to the office, Priscilla handed
McCoy a large envelope.

"Looks like the new orders have arrived," Priscilla
said.

McCoy tore open the big envelope and let the pages
slide out on Priscilla's desk. There were three groups
of papers pinned together. On top was the customary
careful script of the general's secretary who wrote all
of the orders.

McCoy quickly scanned the first sheet. He grunted
and flipped to the second group of papers, then to the
pinned together third group. There he stopped. Clipped
to each of four sheets of paper was one brand-new $20
bill.

"Counterfeiting case," McCoy said. "You were
right." He handed her one of the sheets with the
bill on it. "Is that a good note or funny money?"

She stared at it. "The plate is perfect. I can find no
mistakes, no shading, no lack of detail. It looks genuine,
but the final test is the paper." She lifted the edge of the
bill and rubbed it between her fingers, then she folded
it and slowly shook her head.

"No, it's not legal tender. I'd guess that the plate is
genuine but the paper is not government issue. Not one
in a thousand people can tell a bill printed like this is a
counterfeit."

Spur settled down and read the orders again.

"Spur McCoy, St. Louis Office. Enclosed all material we have on the activity of one Flavian Kirby, age 61, retired engraver from the U.S. Mint here in Washington D.C. When he left he stole engraving plates of both sides of a $20 bill. They are the exact size as a $20 federal bank note.

"Copies of the bills are enclosed. He is a master printer as well and moves around the country setting up his printing plant, grinding off as much money as he needs, then moving on. He is not trying to get rich or flood the country with this bogus money, but he must be stopped.

"As Miss Flanders will tell you, these bills are extremely hard to spot as counterfeit. The best weapon we have against them is the serial number. Each of the bills has the same number, which is 338605438. This is the only sure way a nonexpert can spot the bills. We have notified all banks and financial institutions in your area to be on the lookout for such counterfeit bills.

"Our investigators here tell us that Kirby has moved to St. Louis. In a town of 200,000 people it will be easier to find him than it was in Chicago.

"The man in question is five-feet-four, bearded, unkempt, always wears a dirty, misshapen town hat, uses spectacles all the time, is not given to wild spending sprees. His one easiest spotted vice is the ladies. He is given to the use of prostitutes and has an amazing appetite for a man of his age. He enjoys the most expensive whores in town, so be on the lookout at any fancy parlors that may be open there.

"All banks are cooperating and will give you notice if they find any such bills. Some smaller banks will scan all $20 bills for this number.

"Kirby is believed to be in your city at this time. Expend all possible energy to track him down and arrest him. Is known to be armed at all times with a sword in a cane, a derringer attached to a gold watch fob and concealed in an enlarged vest pocket, and a second derringer in an ankle holster on his right leg.

"Approach with extreme caution. The government wants this man to be taken alive and put on trial to discourage other employees from stealing from the U.S Bureau of Engraving and Printing.

"Other details on the case are enclosed."

McCoy read the rest of the material which was just background on the suspect, his work record, his retirement and the subsequent discovery of the lost plate. Agent Flanders read the reports when McCoy finished with them. She then compared the new $20 bills. She took one off the paper, rubbed away the spot of glue, wadded the bill up into a ball, then spread it out. She took a $20 bill from her own reticule and did the same thing.

The counterfeit did not flatten out as well nor return to its original shape as well as the genuine one.

"The paper he's using is a little too stiff. He knows it, of course, but he can't find the same paper the government uses. It's a special formula by a company in Maine, and the firm is bound by law to sell this particular paper to no one else."

"So we have the crushability and the serial number to go by," McCoy said. "I don't see how this is going to be any big problem."

Agent Flanders still frowned. "This bill is so damned good that not even an experienced teller at a bank will be able to tell by the feel. I'd say we have a big problem, unless we get lucky. Where do we start?"

McCoy scowled and shook his head. "Damnnit, Flanders, you're the expert on counterfeiting. You're here to help, so suppose you tell me where we start."

Priscilla Quincy looked up in wonder.

Chapter Four

Agent Jessica Flanders looked at Spur McCoy to be sure he was serious. She saw that he was and picked up a pencil and a pad of paper from her desk.

"The usual procedures have been started. The Treasury Department has notified all of the bank and financial groups in this area about the chances of counterfeiting, and the banks will make random checks on twenty dollar bills.

"I'd suggest we visit the five or six biggest banks ourselves to go through their twenties and see if we can find anything."

McCoy frowned, then lifted his hand to stop her.

"What if we did find a twenty with this serial number and knew it was a fake? How would a bank know who had deposited it, and if they even found out that, how would the depositor know where he got the bill—if it was a large store, say, or even a saloon?"

"That's the next problem. First we find the bogus bills, then we try to tie down where they came from."

McCoy nodded and stood. "Sounds reasonable. Agent Flanders, you check the banks. Plenty of time to get to the six or seven largest ones before closing time. I'm going to work it from the other end."

Agent Flanders looked up and wrinkled her brow. "I don't quite understand, Mr. McCoy. Which other end are you going to investigate?"

"Specifically I'm going to look for Mr. Flavian Kirby himself and try to find out if anyone has seen him. The best way to do that is to see if he's been a customer at any one of the four or five best parlors in St. Louis. That's the end I'm going to cover, Miss Flanders."

Spots of red peppered Priscilla's face and neck as she blushed and ducked her head. Agent Flanders didn't even blink.

"Yes, good idea, and I'd say you're just the man for the job. You can come and go easily from such establishments without arousing any suspicion."

She slipped on her hat, pinned it in place and marched toward the door. "Oh, in case you wondered, I worked up a list of the biggest banks in town yesterday so I'm all ready to get started. I'll take one of these bogus bills with me to show the bankers. I'm sure you'll have no trouble finding the parlors." She swept out the door and closed it more forcefully than was needed.

Priscilla stood there with her fists on her hips. "McCoy, you certainly weren't nice to your new partner. I'm surprised she so much as speaks to you.

You didn't even make sure she had accommodations last night. Fortunately she's staying here at the hotel. You seem to forget sometimes that women are people, too. Miss Flanders has feelings just like anyone else."

McCoy grinned and chuckled. "Damn, I must have been rough on her if you're standing up and scolding me this way. All right, I'll go easy. Remember, she wasn't my idea, I didn't ask for any help, so you just keep that in mind."

He grabbed his hat and settled it on his head. "Like I told you, I'm going to check out the fancy parlors. Three or four of them popped up lately that the town fathers are not quite sure how to handle. You catch the mail today. Looks like you'll be working right here in the office for some time now, young lady."

"I'm pleased. I'll go through the mail carefully." Her pout was gone, and she grinned again. It was more like the old Pris that he knew.

McCoy started at the top. It was called the St. Louis Club, or usually just the Club, and it was a membership operation that had the best food, best bar and best whores in town. You bought a membership at the door for each visit at a $3 fee. It was not a cheap whorehouse.

He knew that most arrangements were made to use the Club in advance either by the new fancy messenger service that they had between four of the major hotels and the appointment office in the Club or simply by letter.

The Club was on a side street just two blocks from the main thoroughfare of Olive Street. It had no red lights, no big banners or signs. The only identification was the number 333 and the small brass plate on the door which read, THE CLUB.

McCoy had known the owner of the Club for over five years. She was a woman of intelligence, remarkable business sense, good taste, and above all a knack for providing a gentleman with the entertainment and amusement that he wanted most—sex, drink and fine food. She had begun as a whore, saved her money, bought her own bordello, expanded and then made enough profits to interest some investors in establishing the Club. It was a favorite of the gamblers from the river boats.

He knocked on the door. A sliding panel a foot square opened, and a man in a formal dinner jacket, shirt and black tie stared at him a moment. His name was Rhodenway. He smiled, nodded and closed the panel. The heavy oak door swung inward, and McCoy stepped inside the small lobby. It had carpeting two inches thick and expensive and fancy wallpaper. Three original oil paintings hung in prominent places. There were a half dozen luxurious sofas, settees and love seats around the sides of the room.

Rhodenway's formal clothes were immaculate as usual. His smile was warmer now. "Ah, yes, Mr. McCoy. Miss Melissa would be overjoyed to see you. I gather that you're here on business and not for pleasure?"

"Quite right, Rhodenway. I appreciate your fine memory. As I recall, I've only been inside twice before. Exceptionally kind of you to remember."

The tall, dignified man did not respond to the compliment. Instead he turned, motioned to McCoy and led him down a short hallway to a room at the front of the building. Rhodenway knocked on the door once, paused and then tapped three more times.

A girl in her late teens answered the door. McCoy had never seen her before. She smiled sweetly and wore a dress that cost twice a month's pay for a working man.

"Right this way, sir. Miss Melissa is in her private office. Whom should I say is calling?"

"Spur McCoy. I only need ten minutes of her time."

The girl nodded and hurried away. It gave him time to examine the room. It was an entryway, no more than eight feet square, yet furnished as if it were in a palace with a thick carpet and paintings on the wall that looked like nothing he had ever seen before. One was four feet square and had a woman with three arms and three breasts and the body of an alligator. The man in the picture was breathing fire and had six legs but the torso and the head of a human. McCoy shook his head in amazement. Either he was going crazy or some artist was far ahead of his time.

The young girl came back and led him into a luxurious apartment. This sitting room had all sorts of upholstered furniture set in small groups as if several people were having different conversations. The room was elegant, and at the far end on a pure white couch sat a woman in a startling red dress.

"Yes, dear boy. I haven't seen you in some time. How is everything going with the secret service these days?"

The woman speaking was Miss Melissa. No one had ever known her last name. She was now in her mid-forties but was sleek and slender as a girl in her teens. Only her face gave her away. She wore so little makeup that he hardly knew she had any on.

"Come, come, don't stand there gawking like a schoolboy. You must have business. You always have business when you come to see me at the expense of my sexual fantasies. What is it this time?"

Quickly he told her about the counterfeiter and his special tastes. McCoy painted the picture much bleaker than it actually was.

"This man could flood the town with bogus money which will all be returned to the depositor. Every deposit will be checked at every bank for any of those twenties, and when they are found they will be deducted from the total and returned. If he uses your establishment and spends wildly, it could cost you a thousand dollars a day if he isn't stopped."

"Dear boy, I've seen funny money before. I can spot it, and my bookkeeper can spot it."

McCoy took out of his pocket two $20 bills. Both were new, unused. He laid them on the couch beside Miss Melissa.

"Which one is counterfeit?"

She looked at them, picked them up, rubbed them, folded them, then laid them down.

"It's a trick. Neither of them is fake. Both are as good and solid as a double gold eagle."

McCoy took out another of the bogus bills and laid it beside the first two. "Check the serial numbers. Have you ever seen two bank notes with the same serial number before?"

"Of course not." She frowned, then she picked up the two bills with the same number and stared. "But they look so good. The engraving is perfect." She nodded. "If this guy feels like it, he can print himself up a billion dollars worth of twenties and never get caught. The only damn way to spot them would be that serial number."

She put down the bills. "What do you want me to do?"

"The man is a little over sixty, but loves to make love. We understand he utilizes the best houses in whatever town he's working. We have reason to believe he's here in St. Louis, or soon will be. I at once thought of you. Where better for a man to spend all that easily printed money than at the Club?"

She preened herself for a moment, then smiled. "Naturally. We have the best reputation, the best in decor, the best privacy, the best in drink and wine and food. Of course we also offer the most elegant, the most beautiful, the youngest and the hottest young pussies in town. Who do we watch for?"

He gave her the description of the man.

"Not a chance. He'd never get past Rhodenway."

"He would if you told Rhodenway to watch for him and to be sure to let him in. We not only want him, but we need to recover those two plates, the front and back of the twenty dollar bill. We'd be pleased if you would talk to Rhodenway, explain it to him, then send someone to my office or my hotel room when he shows up.

"We won't touch him at your place, but we will follow him back to wherever he's staying and hope we can recover the plates."

"Done. Let me go down and talk to Rhodenway for a moment then I'll be back. Can I offer you anything? Have you had your lunch yet? Yes, we call our noon meal here lunch. Be surprised how many lunches we serve along with the special desert on her backside." Miss Melissa chortled as she swept out of the room.

McCoy sat in one of the upholstered chairs and tried to figure what this master counterfeiter would do.

By now he knew that there must be dozens of law enforcement agencies and city cops after him. Chicago alone would put a fire on his tailfeathers if they ever caught him.

Hell, he would have to change something, the first of which would be his appearance—not his habits but his looks. Gone would be the beard, and he'd have the best suit of clothes his bogus money could buy, instead of his old rags. He'd go slow spending the 20s where they could be traced.

A man buys a 50 cent item and gets change for a counterfeit $20 bill. That leaves him with $19.50 of real money he can spend anywhere without leaving a trace. Say he peddled $1000 of those funny bills in Chicago and came away with $900 in U.S. currency. A man could do a heap of living on $900 without spending another of those tainted bills.

The average store clerk earned about $450 a year if he was lucky. Money went a long ways.

The more he thought about it, the more McCoy decided that Flavian Kirby wouldn't play it quite that conservative. Stealing the plates, printing up the money and fooling the government was one thing. Now he had a record of outfoxing the authorities. That would be where the fun lay for him now.

Flavian would go right on spending his bogus money and feel the thrill of getting away with it. He'd change his appearance but not his habits. That was why McCoy knew he had to get out to the three or four other top social clubs and have them keep a watch for the $20 bills. He wrote the serial number of the counterfeit $20 on a pad of paper and had it ready when Miss Melissa came back.

"Now, our staff is ready and waiting to find this counterfeiter for you. I've arranged to have a light lunch here for you and Evette, and even if you don't wish to stay after the meal, Evette will understand."

"Miss Melissa, I appreciate your kindness and hospitality, but I have a dozen more people to alert about this hombre, and I just can't take the time right now. Maybe I could take a rain check from you on that offer."

Miss Melissa cocked her head to one side as a girl stepped into the sitting room. She wore a thin, silk, pink robe that almost wasn't there. It revealed in stunning clarity surging breasts, a swatch of darkness at her crotch and a shower of dark brown hair that came just below her shoulders.

"Sorry, Evette, maybe later," McCoy said. He was sweating by the time he made it to the door, and he was sure that Evette had seen the start of a bulge behind his fly. What sacrifices he made for the good of the secret service!

McCoy talked to the owners or managers of the other three parlors. None was as flashy or as well-appointed as the Club, but each had a clientele and worked hard at providing food, drink and girls in any order that wa. desired. All agreed to cooperate fully in watching for Flavian Kirby and the bogus bills.

By the time he got down to the fifth name on his list he was into the bordellos, where the madams were quicker to deal with. He said he'd see to it that any of the $20 bills with the right serial number on it would be fully refunded, if he was notified about it within two or three hours after it was found.

He left the bad bill number everywhere he went and even told the café owner where he had lunch about it. By 4:00 o'clock he had covered the 23 largest whorehouses in town. He wasn't sure how many there were left. The St. Louis City Council had been trying to close up the raunchiest of them but had little success. The Mississippi River boat traffic had pegged St. Louis as a major sex capital, and it was a title hard to get rid of.

By the time McCoy made it back to the office, it was nearly five in the afternoon. Priscilla was still there.

"Not much in the mail. Another wire from the general is on your desk."

He slouched behind the unpolished oak and ripped open the wire.

"TO: SPUR MCCOY, CAPITAL INVEST-IGATIONS, CLAYMORE HOTEL, ST. LOU-IS, MISSOURI. TODAY RECEIVED COM-PLAINT FROM JEFFERSON SPRINGS, MIS-SOURI, ABOUT THE JEFFERSON SPRINGS BANK ISSUING ITS OWN PAPER CUR-RENCY. THEY ARE IN DENOMINATIONS OF $1, $5 AND $10. NO OTHER BANK KNOWN TO BE IN THAT GENERAL AREA. STATE OF MISSOURI NO LONGER CHARTERS BANKS TO ISSUE CURREN-CY. FOLLOW-UP ON THIS AS QUICK-

LY AS POSSIBLE AS TIME PERMITS ON THE MORE URGENT COUNTERFEITING ASSIGNMENT. KEEP ME INFORMED OF PROGRESS ON BOTH PROJECTS WITH REPORTS AT LEAST WEEKLY. SENDING: GEN. W. D. HALLECK, WASHINGTON, D.C."

McCoy looked up and scowled at Priscilla. "You hear of any more of those phony banks printing up their own money any more? Lots of it back in the fifties and sixties. I haven't heard of any lately."

"I saw something in one of the newspapers about it yesterday. I can try and find the article for you."

"Please do that. Any word from our lady agent?"

"We had lunch together. So far she hadn't found any of the fake twenties. She figured she would keep at it until the last bank closed at five."

"I might send her out to Jefferson City to look into this bank swindle." He gave the telegram to Priscilla. "I figured that all of these old shysters had been caught by now. Wonder how this one slipped through for so long?"

"It seems to me the newspaper said it was a new bank that seemed to be doing just fine, making loans, cashing checks, everything. I know I have the article at home."

"Bring it in tomorrow."

"How did your afternoon go in the bawdy houses?"

"I'm so tired I can hardly walk."

Priscilla looked up, those pink spots blossoming on her cheeks again.

"Don't believe it. I left that serial number at twenty-seven different establishments. If he's in town, we should have him spotted soon."

The door opened and a grinning Jessica Flanders pranced into the room holding a well-worn bank note in her hand.

"Breakthrough. I just found one of the bogus twenties at the Landowners Bank of St. Louis."

Chapter Five

Spur McCoy looked up at Agent Flanders. "You found the first bogus twenty. Good. Who deposited it?"

Jessica shook her head. "It was in the cash drawer of one of the tellers, but the young man said he'd handled thirty or forty of the twenty dollar bills today and had no idea if he took it in today or if it had been in his cash drawer for three days. That's when he took over the window and took out all new bills from the vault."

"Does he handle any big stores or industrial accounts?"

"I didn't ask."

"Tomorrow, as soon as they open, get a list of his customers for the past three days. Some banks keep records like that when drafts are cashed. See if you can find any of the bordellos on the list."

"I'll do that. I'm having a notice printed to distribute to every bank and every store in town asking them to be on the lookout for this special twenty dollar bill. If we can get everyone watching for it . . ."

McCoy shook his head. "No, not a good idea. All that will do is force Flavian to spend the real money he's taken in when he changed a fake twenty. That won't help us. It could also put him on a train or boat out of town. We need the notices but only for specific stores and banks.

"The bordellos are checking every twenty they take in before they accept it. All of the banks should be checking every twenty they get over the counter. That should be your message for them tomorrow."

Jessica nodded slowly. "Yes, I see what you mean. We don't want to scare him away now that we know he's in town."

"We don't know that for sure yet, Miss Flanders. Someone from Chicago who took in one of his bogus marks might have come through St. Louis and spent it, but I'd say the odds are that he's here.

"One more minor problem. Flavian has been passing bogus money for nearly six months now. He knows that a thousand lawmen are looking for him. If you were in his place, Miss Flanders, what would you do?"

"Change his appearance. Shave off his beard and moustache, trim his hair close, buy some conservative and well-fitting clothes. That would give him a much different look."

"I figure that's about what he's done. It's easier to change your clothes and shave off a beard than it is to change your habits. I'd say the parlors and bordellos are still our best bet of snagging him."

Agent Flanders sighed. "I guess you're right. Tomorrow I'll go see all of the banks in town and give them my flyer that has the number of the bill on it. That could improve our chances. Some of these banks might not want to be bothered to check each twenty, but most of them don't take in that many big bills."

McCoy pushed the telegram over to the new agent. "What do you make of this?"

When she read it she frowned. "Strange. Most of those fake banks were routed out of business ten years ago. How can this one pop up like this with all the new state regulations?"

"It's beyond me; that's your area. Why don't you take a run out there to Jefferson Springs tomorrow and see what you can find out?"

"But what about the counterfeiting case here?"

"Seems the general has given us two assignments that kind of overlap. Tell you what. You catch the 8:05 train west tomorrow, and I'll cover the banks for you. That way we can double up on the work and get moving on the new assignment. Could be a few days before we get anything more on our counterfeiter. This bank deal could ruin a lot of honest folks out in Jefferson Springs if it isn't dealt with quickly."

"Right. I've read about how they operate. Back in the sixties they issued money, great looking bills, some even in different colors. One of these so-called banks they ran down had as its only assets a rented room, a barrel stove and one chair."

"Sounds reasonable, so that's your assignment for tomorrow. Get some travel money from Pris and best plan to stay overnight. See if any of that outfit is left and do what needs doing. Wire us if you have any problems."

"Yes sir," Jessica said. "Oh, I had a message for you. I talked to the owner of the St. Louis State Bank. She said your account was overdue and that you should stop in for a conference as soon as possible to keep your credit rating. I'm not sure what she meant by that."

Priscilla looked away and became busy at her desk.

"Yes, thanks, I'll take care of it. Now, I'd say it's near quitting time, so if you ladies will excuse me, I'll be calling it a day."

"No night duty at the pleasure palaces?" Jessica asked with a tinge of irony in her voice.

"Later on. They don't get moving until the dinner trade after six. Evening, ladies."

Spur moved through the connecting door into his room and slid the bolt home on the inside. So, Lucinda wanted to see him again. Fine, but he probably should be working the whore houses. Hell, he didn't know how big this Flavian Kirby was on dining out. He might just utilize the parlors for the girls and the drinks. With some proper timing he could take care of both small tasks.

Spur stripped off his shirt, gave himself a sponge bath to the waist, scrubbed his face and shaved again to get things down to the pink. Then he combed his hair, slapped on a little bay rum and rose water on his face to cut the sting, then put on a pair of town pants, a matching brown shirt, a string tie and a soft brown jacket. He felt dressed up enough to haunt one or two of the parlors or Lucinda's town apartment.

He checked her bank, but everyone was gone. A short walk later he lifted the knocker on her apartment door and was rewarded with quick steps inside and the door coming open.

Lucinda stood there. "Spur, you got my message." She pulled him inside, kissed him wetly and then motioned to the table set for two. "I figured a girl has to compete with those damn parlors, so here it is—dinner, the finest bourbon in St. Louis and for desert, me."

She had brought her cook in from the other house and prepared a gourmet feast—squab, small steaks, a fish dish along with half a dozen vegetables, wine and coffee. McCoy ate until he could barely roll out of his chair. They watched the sunset outside her window, then hurried into the bedroom.

"McCoy, you're ungrateful for all I'm giving you. Do you know that? Why don't you give up and settle down and marry me and make an honest woman of me so I can join polite society again?"

He grinned. It was a little ritual they went through almost every time. He knew his lines.

"Because you really don't want to get married. Because you'd rather feel sexy and raunchy and have somebody like me grab you and kiss you like this."

He kissed her deep, his tongue almost getting lost in her throat.

When it ended she relaxed in his arms and stared up at him.

"Besides, you want somebody to rip off your blouse, fondle your fine breasts, slowly set them on fire and make your nipples throb with fresh, hot new blood."

As he said it he opened the buttons down the front of her blouse, then pushed away her chemise and attacked her breasts with both his hands and his mouth.

By now, Lucinda was gasping. She could hardly talk. When she pointed to the bed, he carried her there, putting her down gently. Her legs stretched wide, and her knees came up, billowing her skirt around her waist. She wore nothing under it.

"Yes, yes, yes, McCoy, I'll marry you for tonight, but just for tonight. Now get on with it before I melt!"

In a modest but fancy hotel halfway across town, a man of five-feet-four inches considered himself in the mirror. Yes, a fantastic change. Anyone hunting him now would have a devil of a time recognizing him. His face was clean-shaven, done in three stages by himself, so there would be no witnesses here in St. Louis. His face still stung from the razor, but the results were gratifying. He found two small brown patches on one cheek he never knew were there. Liver spots some called them. So he was 61; what did he expect? He combed his hair with care. It had been years since it had been this short, a regular business-man's haircut, short on the sides with a part down the right side.

He slipped on the pair of glasses he had bought at a variety store. They had thick hornrims on them but were pure glass inside. He polished the glass and could see as well as always. His eyesight had always been excellent. Forty years as an engraver had not dulled his vision.

Now he set a sporty soft-billed cap on his head. It was made of wool and would be warm to cover his balding spot, but it also gave him a rakish look.

Once more he checked over his clothing. The suit was new, the latest fashion from New York. He had found himself suddenly short of honest cash and had to spend one of the Kirby Twenties, as he called them, but it had been worth it. The suit was a deep blue with just the hint of a pinstripe.

His shoes were the finest leather and were black to match the suit. Satisfied with his appearance, he checked a locked valise that he had put under the bed. Inside were banded bundles of bills, Kirby Twenties. He knew exactly how much he had left—$88,380. He kept track where and when he spent the bogus bills, partly so he would know where to travel next and partly so he would know when he needed to find a spot to set up a small print shop. In Chicago he had simply bought a one-man shop that was for sale, took over the press and at night printed out his new supply of Kirby Twenties.

He looked in an envelope marked U.S. bills. In the big envelope was the legitimate Silver Certificates issued by his old boss the Bureau of Engraving and Printing. He didn't have an exact count of this cash. He had left Chicago with about $1,200, and most of it was still there.

He took out $60 and put it in his wallet which fit neatly in the back pocket of his new suit. That should be enough for an evening at one of the lavish new whorehouses he had heard about. They were the main reason he had come to St. Louis. Food, drink and sex all at the same table!

Kirby went downstairs, caught a cab and gave the address, 333 Boundary St. The cabby gave him a grin.

"Hope you got an appointment. That place has been busy as hell tonight. Must be payday or something."

At the door of the Club, the panel opened and Rhodenway stared out. He continued to look at the small man outside.

"The name is Amway. I have an appointment for 6:15 tonight."

A moment later the panel closed and the door opened. Rhodenway motioned to a young girl seated on one of the sofas.

"Mr. Amway to 604," he said sharply.

The girl nodded, hooked her hand through his arm and led him down the hallway. There was no elevator here. They climbed to the sixth floor and to room 604. She stopped and watched him for a moment.

"Business before dinner," the girl said softly. She held out a silver tray just long enough to hold paper currency. On it was a slip of paper with the figure $45. The short man reached in his pocket, took out his wallet, placed two U.S. printed twenties and a five on the tray and put away his wallet. At these prices there would be no tips. This had better be good. The girl smiled, tucked the tray and the money under her arm and knocked on the door twice.

When Flavian Kirby looked around, the winsome girl was gone. The door opened and another lovely stood there. She was an inch shorter than he was, as he had proscribed, blonde with long hair and on the chunky side just the way he liked them. The girl smiled.

"Mr. Amway, I'm Delphine. Please come in, and I'll have our dinner sent right up. You ordered the roast pheasant, wild rice and stuffing along with a fine port wine. Everything should be ready."

His eyes bulged. He'd never seen a whore who looked like this. She could have been at a society ball or at the President's inauguration. She was beautiful, hair perfect, surging breasts almost covered by a clinging silk gown. Her waist was ample and the gown was cut short, mid-thigh as he had ordered. He wanted to jump on top of her right there.

The large room had soft carpeting, finely decorated wallpaper, oil and watercolor paintings on the wall, elegant furnishings, a big open window with a river view and a small dining table to the left near the window. It was luxurious.

"I know you're anxious. Let me ring for the order, then we can get better acquainted before the meal arrives."

She went to a pull cord and tugged on it four times. A moment later she led him to a double bed, exquisitely covered with a spread with what he swore must be gold threads.

When she sat down on the bed, the gown slipped open, revealing one of her large breasts.

"My dear!"

Delphine smiled. "You just go right ahead and enjoy. Whatever you want, I want. You can have some small bites if you wish."

He bent and kissed the glowing orb. A dozen kisses later he licked the nipple and felt it surge upward.

"My goodness, you really know what you want, Mr. Amway."

A knock on the door interrupted them. She pushed her breast beneath the fabric, stood up and walked across the thick carpet to the door.

A young girl in a white tunic that was skintight rolled a cart into the room. She was dark-eyed, black-haired and slender as a reed. She pushed the cart to the dining table set for two and set out the covered dishes and the chilled bottle of wine.

Then she bowed, pushed the cart out of the room and left without a word.

Delphine went to the bed where the man slowly rubbed a lump behind his pants's fly.

"Dinnertime, Mr. Amway. Then we do whatever you want to do for the rest of the night." She paused. "You should seat me now, Mr. Amway."

He jumped to her side, pulled out a chair, let her ease into it and then pushed it forward to the table. Kirby took his place opposite her as Delphine uncovered the chafing dishes.

"Oh, roast pheasant! I just love it." She used a knife and fork and quickly carved the bird into half a dozen pieces.

"Which piece to start with? A breast or a drumstick?"

The dinner was a smashing success. Kirby proved he could hold his wine, and finally he was filled to his limit.

"A short nap," he said. "I want your tits to be my pillow."

She slipped out of the robe and, naked, led him to the bed. He kissed her breasts and nibbled at them, then positioned her slantwise across the big bed. He slid out of his shoes and jacket and lay down with his head nestled on her bountiful breasts.

"I'm in heaven," he said. His eyes closed, and a moment later he was sleeping.

He awoke with a start less than five minutes later. Something had bothered his slumber. Then he felt it again. Delicate fingers had opened his fly, worked through his underwear and had brought him to a full erection while he snoozed with his head cushioned on her breasts.

"Sonofabitch," he whispered. "Nobody's ever done me that way before. You're good, Delphine, damn good."

She undressed him, and when they sat side by side on the big featherbed, she kissed his cheek gently, then smiled sweetly at him.

"Mr. Amway, just what kind of sexy games do you want to play now?"

Chapter Six

Flavian Kirby, going by the name of Amway, faced the most beautiful woman he'd ever seen sitting stark naked on the bed beside him.

"What kind of sexy games do I want to play?" he asked. "Hell, all of them. You can start by stripping me naked. I do love to have a sexy, naked woman undress me."

"What about this big fellah down here?" Delphine asked. She stroked his stiff cock and then bent and kissed its purple head.

"Hell, he'll just have to wait his fucking turn."

Delphine moved quickly, straddling his torso and sitting on his lap. Slowly she brushed her breasts against his jacket, then slid it off his arms. Next she attacked his vest and his shirt until he was naked to the waist.

Delphine pushed him down gently to the bed and moved higher, lowering one of her breasts into his mouth.

"Glory!" was all he had a chance to say before he was overcome with a warm, marvelous tit filling his mouth. He chewed and licked it, and when he was about to yelp, she pulled that breast out and slipped the other one in.

"Some men don't like to suck tits, but I think you do. Later you can be on top and really eat my girls right down to a nub." As he mouthed her breast, she pulled his pants and long underwear down around his knees.

She stood up and took off his new town shoes, his socks, and then his trousers and long johns.

She urged him to slide up on the bed, then she began kissing his feet, playing with his toes with one hand and gently stroking his rock hard cock with the other.

"Woman, what the hell you doing?" Kirby yelped.

"Getting you ready for the best fuck you've ever had. Isn't that what you want?"

She didn't wait for an answer. She worked up his leg with her hand, massaging and kneading. She came to his balls and fingered them a moment.

Her head then went between his legs, and she licked his balls until he whimpered.

"No, no more I'm almost ready to shoot!"

She lifted her head, stroked him twice with her hand, then mouthed his cock and pumped twice more with her mouth, enveloping most of him until he screeched like a wounded mountain lion.

His hips bucked upward half a dozen times, and she accepted all he had. He panted like a two-mile-run horse and stared at her in amazement. It took him three minutes to get his breathing under control so he could talk.

"How'd you make me come so fast? I'm sixty-one years-old, for God's sakes. I ain't no quick erupting fourteen year-old never been sucked-off virgin."

She smiled and lay down beside him. "You want to use my pussy for a pillow while you get your strength back?"

He shook his head. "Tits again. Damn but you got a fine set of big tits. I'm more a tit man than a leg lover anyway."

She moved so he could lay his head on her breasts, and he sighed. "Goddamn, this is starting out good."

"Tell me, Mr. Amway, what is the one thing you wish you could do to a woman, or you'd like a woman to do to you that you've never got up nerve enough to ask for?"

"Lordy, I've done about everything."

"A stand-up fuck?"

"Done that."

"Us both eating each other at the same time, end to end?"

"Tried that, but you done your half already."

"How about fucking me when I'm standing on my head?"

"Never tried that."

She laughed, rolled off him onto her back and pulled him with her. "Good, because it won't work—the wrong angles." She spread her legs and caught his cock and worked on it until it came rock hard again.

"Inside me, quickly. If we're going to get in five fucks before midnight we have to hurry."

"Why midnight? I bought the whole night."

"Of course, Mr. Amway, but after midnight we sleep for two hours, wake up and try something new. We also get a late night dinner at two A.M. You wouldn't want to miss that would you?"

He lifted away from her, crawled between her sleek thighs, aimed for her heartland—and missed. She giggled, put down one hand and helped him find the right slot. He plunged into her twat like an arrow into water.

"Oh, yeah!" Amway shouted. "Now this is what enjoying life is all about. Great food, good cocksucking and now a fuck that won't let me quit."

Delphine brought her legs up and circled them around his torso, locking them together. Then her arms banded like steel around his back and she started humping him, grabbing him with her pussy muscles, then letting him almost slide out before capturing his prick again.

"Lord oh Lord, but are you good. Nobody ever milked me that way before. How did you learn to do that so fucking good?"

She smiled at him in the soft lamp light. "Practice, Mr. Amway. I'm the best because I do a lot of practicing."

She was bucking against him harder now, and before he realized it, he had climaxed again. When the last thrusts of his hips had finished he sagged on top of her, so exhausted he could hardly move.

It was five minutes this time before he could talk. He looked at her and rolled away. "Glory! I don't know when I've been fucked so damn wonderful."

"I'd say never, Mr. Amway. This is Delphine, and I'm the highest price girl in the stable here. Everything I do is the best. You want a full body massage?"

Without waiting for his response, she rolled him over on his stomach, and starting with his arms over his head, she worked his hands and fingers and relaxed each set

of muscles before moving on. She had both arms done
and went to work on his shoulders when she realized he
was asleep.

At once she got up, went to the window and opened
it, letting the cold October air rush in. She closed the
window and stood there watching the street below. He
was too old. Maybe once more and he'd be through for
the night. He might even miss the two o'clock late dinner. Delphine was damn certain that she wouldn't miss
it. A working girl in this business had to keep up her
strength.

She watched him sleeping. He wouldn't wake up
until morning if she let him snooze. She went to his
trousers, checked the pockets and found more than
$200 in what looked like new bills. They were under
a little flap that was supposed to hide them, but she'd
seen every kind of wallet ever made.

She was tempted. Delphine could use another $200
in her Oregon fund. When she had enough cash saved,
she would steam out of this St. Louis so fast she'd leave
it spinning. Next she'd grab the train in Omaha and be
in Oregon before she knew it. Oregon! It had a magic
ring to it. She'd never been there, but she knew two girls
who had. They said it rained a lot, but that made the
country so green it must look like the Emerald Island of
Ireland.

Delphine left the window and nibbled at some of
the cold pheasant. She salted the leftover drumstick and chewed all of the meat off it. Back
to work.

She eased Amway over onto his back and worked
on his flaccid tool. Quickly she had him hard again.

He moaned in his sleep, humped his hips once and smiled.

She woke him when the late dinner came at 2:00 A.M. He was groggy for a while, but the wine revived him, and the spicy sausages and chicken wings and little cherry cakes were more than enough to get him fully awake.

When they finished eating, she rolled the small cart out of the room and locked the door. In her most tempting naked way, Delphine swayed as she walked back to where he sat on the bed. She waltzed her fur muff right up to his chin and brushed it against his lips.

"Damn, I'd love to, but twice a night is my limit. I'm so washed out not even you could get me up for another go around. I might as well get dressed and go back to my hotel. I'm at an age where I need my sleep."

Delphine nodded. She'd been expecting as much. "Usually if a man's happy with my work, he makes a small donation to my retirement fund."

He grinned. "Delphine, you'll never retire, not with a hot little cunt like yours. But I can afford to turn a twenty your way. Will that help?"

She jumped on his lap, hugged him, kissed his cheek, then beamed at him. "That would just be ever so grand. You must promise to come back and see me tomorrow, maybe in the afternoon." She helped him dress and walked arm in arm with him to the secluded side entrance where they had a cab waiting for him.

When Delphine reported to Miss Melissa that she was available again, she said nothing about the $20 bill that Flavian Kirby had given her. He had reached in the wrong compartment and given her one of the counterfeits.

Delphine went back to her own room, eased the floorboard up and took out a small metal box in which she kept her traveling money. She put the bogus $20 bill along with the rest of her stashed loot. She didn't have to count it. She knew that with this $20 she now had $1,435. When she got to an even $2,000 she was heading for Portland.

Spur McCoy left Lucinda's apartment at 6:30 the next morning while the banker slept. It was their usual pattern. He gave his face and torso a quick sponge bath and dressed, then hurried down to a café for coffee, his first cigar and breakfast.

Today he would check all the banks again and urge them to look over every $20 bill they handled. It would be quite a task. He picked up the printed flyers and circled the bogus serial number on each of them.

He had Jessica's list from the office. There were 22 banking and financial establishments in Denver. He talked to all but three before the day was over and got back to the office just before 4:00 that afternoon.

Priscilla was on the job. "Jessica got off on the 8:05 for Jefferson City. She wired from there that she had arrived and was starting to hunt for the suspects. How did you do today with all of your banker friends?"

He told her that he had damn near talked his mouth off all day long.

"We've had no reports of fake twenty dollar bills from any of the pleasure palaces," Priscilla said. "At least none today which would be from their take last night. Either they aren't watching for the serial number on the bill or our man didn't spend any fake money yesterday."

"Or the girls and madams missed it." McCoy tossed his hat at his desk. "We don't have a damn thing to go on. Five will get you fifty that Flavian Kirby has changed his appearance, so that's a dead end. How are we going to find this man?"

Priscilla seldom saw McCoy this worried. She frowned at him. "Now don't you go getting upset, Mr. McCoy. You've whipped tougher ones than this. I'm betting that the parlors will be where our first real lead comes from. Oh, did you check that teller who handled the first fake bill?"

"That I did. He's a prissy little sonofabitch who doesn't really want to cooperate with us. His manager made him give me a list of the business firms he serviced during the past three days. That bank keeps a record, but the list I got didn't help. On it were hardware stores, cafés, a livery and even a saddle shop, but not one single bordello."

McCoy sat at his desk and looked at the new mail. Nothing from the general. He pushed it aside. "Anything here I need to look over?"

"Nothing that can't wait. A request from Washington for some more information on one of the old cases. I'll find your report on it tomorrow."

"Fair enough. Why don't you go on home. I'm about to take off myself and call it a wasted day. I'm tired of talking to bankers."

Priscilla looked up quickly and grinned.

"Yes, except for that one lady banker," he said. "Now get out of here. There's a new production at the Variety Theatre on tonight, and I sort of promised that one lady banker that I'd take her to see it."

In Jefferson Springs, Missouri, Secret Service Agent Jessica Flanders stepped off the train and first went to check in with the local lawman.

"Hey, we don't even got a town marshal no more," the man at the General Store told her. Jefferson Springs was little more than a whistle stop, with about 200 people scattered in a long row of houses along the one main street that was half a block over from the railroad tracks.

"How far away is the county sheriff?" she asked.

"Sheriff? Yep, we got one of them, but he's nigh on to twenty-five mile out west a piece. Used to have a deputy here, but nothing ever happened, so the sheriff took him back to the county seat."

"What's the name of the county seat?" Jessica asked.

"That one I know. Forest Grove, over there at the edge of Grove County. Lots of farm folks over that way."

"What was your name again, sir?"

"Me, oh, I'm Hirum Jarek. That last name is Slovakian in case you're interested."

"Good to meet you, Mr. Jarek. Is the post office here in your store?"

"Certainly is, Miss. You have something to mail or need some stamps or something?"

"Just some information. You must know about everyone in town. Can you tell me where I can find the Jefferson Springs Bank? I didn't see it as I walked here from the railroad station just now."

"Bank? Town this size don't got no bank, Miss."

"I'm certain this is the right town. It's called the Jefferson Springs Bank."

The man folded his arms across his chest. He was thin and rangy, and now his face took on a tense, defensive look about it that surprised her.

"Got to be mistaken, Miss. Never been a bank in this town for all the days I been here. I opened the store nigh on to twelve years ago. Must have us mixed up with Jefferson Springs over in Illinois. It happens all the time."

She nodded, but a gnawing doubt creeped into her mind that this wasn't going to be as easy as it first looked.

"Well, thanks for your time. The hotel, just down the street, is still open, isn't it?"

"Sure as rain. My kinfolk run it. They have a batch of nice rooms there, and the café across the street turns out a good mess of fine cooking."

She thanked him and left the store, her small valise still in hand. No bank. Amazing! She hadn't seen the actual fraudulent bank notes, but if they came from Jefferson Springs, Missouri, this was the town. Could it be possible that there was a bank here that no one knew about?

It seemed ridiculous even to consider the idea. One thing struck her as she paced along the boardwalk toward the two-story hotel. If nobody knew about a bank here, none of the local people could have lost any money in it. That was one satisfying thought.

She looked across the street and saw what appeared to her to be a typical bank building. It was solid, conservative and had newspapers pasted over the windows on the inside. From where she stood she could see just the end of some lettering that had been scraped off the window. The last letters that were not quite obliterated were "ank."

She continued to the hotel and checked in. She had a small room, clean and aired out, with sheets and a passable mattress. One chair, a scarred dresser and the usual pitcher full of water and a bowl for washing completed the picture. There was no mirror on the dresser.

She sat on the bed a moment and looked at the small watch she carried on a chain around her neck. It was just past 3:30 in the afternoon. Jessica adjusted her trim brown hat, repinned it, then checked the traveling dress. Yes, it was sufficient for dinner out in a town like this.

She walked down from her second floor room and nodded at the desk clerk but kept the key to her room in her reticule.

She walked north past the General Store, then crossed the street, pausing at every small store and business firm on the way. There were only 15 stores that she counted. She watched a woman working in a dress shop, pinning up cloth on a clothes dummy. The woman glanced up, saw her and nodded.

Two stores later Jessica was in front of the building that could only be a bank. Now it was plain that the lettering across the big front window had been scraped off, probably with a sharp knife or a razor. She could still see the outline of the lettering on the glass. Plainly it said: Jefferson Springs Bank.

Jessica heard something behind her, and when she turned around, the store owner and the woman from the dress shop were so close they hemmed her in against the building. Mr. Jarek, the General Store merchant, held a six-gun aimed at her stomach, almost touching her dress.

"Like I said, Miss, we ain't never had no bank here in Jefferson City, Missouri. You best just come along with us."

Chapter Seven

Spur McCoy had enjoyed the production of *Hamlet* at the Variety Theatre the night before, and after the play the games in the lady banker's big featherbed had been even more invigorating. But with a new morning and his first cup of coffee, he got back to business.

There was no morning telegram from Jessica in Jefferson City. This bothered him some, but he decided she could take care of herself on a little bank scam gone bad like this one. He decided that he should make a tour of the city's ten largest retail stores, tell them about the fake $20 and see if they would cooperate. He was running out of ideas on how to find this counterfeiter.

Before he left the office, a messenger came with a note that he should come to the Missouri State Bank at once. They had found one of the fake bills. He followed the messenger back to the bank where a tall, somber man ushered him into an office.

The name plate on the desk said he was H. Charles Devinger, President.

"Mr. Devinger, you found one of the counterfeit twenties?"

He shook hands with the agent and nodded. "Mr. McCoy, indeed we have. One of my bright young tellers caught it, and she even knows who deposited it." He held out the bill, and McCoy checked the serial number which he had memorized. Then he compared it with one of the counterfeit bills from an envelope in his pocket.

"It's a match, Mr. Devinger. Could I talk to that teller?"

The banker motioned, and a slender young woman came into the room. She was medium sized with boyish hips, and the fit of her dress failed to reveal any sizeable breasts. She had dark hair and brows and a faint hue of color in her skin that suggested perhaps some Indian blood. Her dark eyes danced with excitement, and her smile would light up a coal mine tunnel at midnight.

"Miss Cloud, would you tell Agent McCoy about the deposit?"

"Yes sir. The bill was the only twenty in the cash deposit from a small business I always handle— the Rathmore Clothier Shop. Mr. Rathmore comes in every morning at opening time with the receipts from the day before. I saw the twenty, and it didn't feel right. But all the twenties I've handled since we got the notice don't feel right."

She took a deep breath, and McCoy saw her breasts rise beneath the fabric. That made him feel ever so much better. They were there, just kind of hiding.

"I checked the serial number with the one I wrote down on my pad, and it matched. I showed it to the head teller who said indeed it was the same. He told me to go ahead and accept it and not upset the depositor. I did, and they sent the messenger to your office—and here I am."

"What do you know about this depositor, Miss Cloud?"

"Mr. Rathmore is a sweet man, kind and thoughtful. He's gentle and honest, and I'm sure he didn't know the bill was a fake. It's a well-made counterfeit."

"Could you give me the address of the firm?"

She recited it from memory, and the bank president nodded. "Yes, Mr. McCoy, that's the store. Is there anything else we need to do?"

"No, I'll confiscate this counterfeit bill and put it in one of your bank's envelopes to identify where it came from. You'll deduct it from the deposit, and if possible we'll compensate Mr. Rathmore."

McCoy smiled at Miss Cloud. "I may be back to ask you some more questions later." She nodded and scurried out of the room.

"Your first break in the case, Mr. McCoy?"

"No, we've picked up another bill, but we had no lead as to where it came from. This is our best lead so far." He took the envelope the banker gave him, put the $20 bill inside and shook the man's hand.

"Thanks for your help. Please alert your people to watch for any more such bills. I'm going to go buy myself a new shirt."

McCoy found the small men's clothing store right

where the banker said it would be, and when he stepped inside, he saw that it had only one clerk, probably the owner, Mr. Rathmore himself.

"Yes sir, what can I do for you today?" the man asked. He was smaller than average, dressed immaculately in a conservative mold. He wore spectacles and had thinning gray hair. McCoy figured he was about 50.

McCoy told the clothier why he was there and showed him his identification and badge and then the counterfeit bill.

"Gracious, this is terrible. I had no idea the man wasn't honest. He was dressed well. A conservative suit, good shirt, links in his cuffs, gold watch and chain. Goodness me, will I get in trouble?"

"Not if you cooperate. You do remember who gave you the twenty?"

"Yes, it was the only one I took in yesterday. He bought a new tie, and two pairs of socks and a new vest to go with the suit he wore."

"Can you describe him for me? How tall was he?"

"On the short side, five-feet-four, I'd say. Not heavy, no more than a hundred and twenty pounds. He's one of those men who get thinner as they get older instead of the other way around. My guess is that he's just over sixty years-old. He had bright, clear blue eyes. I tend to notice that sort of thing. They matched his blue suit."

"Did he have any accent?"

"No, not that I recall. Midwestern if any, although I did detect a slight twang of the Maine coast. Yes, it was down east, reminded me of my early days in Boston."

"Any facial hair?"

"Oh, no, cleanly shaven and with some bay rum or such. Quite a spiffy gentleman if you ask me."

"Shoes?"

"Best style. Bet he paid over eight dollars for them. Excellent make of shoe."

"Spiffy, dapper, about sixty, clean-shaven. Did he wear a hat?"

"Curious, he didn't. I'd have expected him to."

"White shirt, stiff collar?"

"Exactly, like he was going to a fancy party or ball or something."

"What time of the day did he come in?"

"Just before I closed at six. In fact he made me a little late getting home for my supper, and my wife was upset."

"Did he have the appearance of going to some event?"

"Yes, he seemed keyed up, excited."

Spur McCoy dug into his wallet, took out a $20 bill and handed it to the clothier. "This is to replace your loss. The bank has deducted the fake twenty from your account. We don't have to replace counterfeit bills, but in this case you've cooperated with me and given us some valuable information, so the government will replace your loss."

McCoy took the man's thanks and hurried out of the store. Now he had a description of the counterfeiter for the whorehouses. It would take him half the day to get around to them. He started with Miss Melissa at the Club.

"Talk to your top girls," McCoy suggested. "See if any of them remember such a man, sixties, five-four, good dresser, might be in a blue suit, blue eyes, gray hair thinning, spiffy dresser and no facial hair."

"Well, now, McCoy, that cuts down the field," Miss Melissa said from where she sat in her office. "Not a lot of men in their sixties visit us. Makes it a lot easier. I'll talk to the girls, and if I find any kind of a match, I'll get a messenger over to your hotel pronto."

Two of the madams refused to talk with him. They seemed to think that if anyone could stiff the government for a few fake $20 bills, so much the better. He plowed along the streets until he had covered the top 20 whorehouses.

He got back to the office foot weary and not as enthusiastic as he had been that morning.

"Nothing new has happened since you've been gone," Priscilla said.

He told her about the match on the bill and the description of the spiffy little man passing it.

"So now you have something to work with," Priscilla said. "Now I know it won't be long. He'll spend more of the bills. Maybe he's run out of his good currency."

"I hope so. Anything from Jessica?"

Priscilla frowned and shook her head. "She said she'd let us know if anything happened one way or another before she started back—at least once a day. We haven't heard anything since she arrived in that little town. It's about eighty miles west?"

"Yes." He furrowed his brow for a moment. "I'm sure she can take care of herself. She's an experienced agent. Why don't you send her a wire to be picked up at the telegraph office. Ask her for a progress report. It should bring a response."

He grabbed his hat. "What time do the banks close now?"

"Usually about four, but then they have to balance and all, so most of the workers don't get away until around five."

"Good. I want to talk to that teller again. You close up at five if I'm not back."

"No night work?" Priscilla asked wistfully.

"Not for you, Pris. You get home and get your rest. Tomorrow might be a tougher day."

He hurried out of the hotel and straight for the Missouri State Bank. It was only four blocks away, so he marched at a brisk pace and arrived just before five. Two workers were leaving the bank by the side door. Someone unlocked the door and let them out, then locked it again. He called out to the two young men.

"Pardon me, but has Miss Cloud left yet? I'm the government man who talked to her this morning."

They stopped and looked at each other, then one of them came back.

"I'm certain she's still here. Something about not balancing. Since you're a lawman I guess it's all right to let you in."

"I have some more questions for her."

The bank teller went back, rapped on the door and spoke with the guard there a moment, then waved McCoy forward.

"Yes, she's still here. We have to sign in and out these days. The guard, Percy, will take you to her window."

Moments later McCoy found Miss Cloud with her chin in her hand. Before she looked up she let out a little cry of joy. "I found it! I found that miserable two dollar mistake!"

"I'm quite glad you found it," McCoy said. She looked up startled and smiled.

"Well, Mr. McCoy. You said you might have some questions for me, but you didn't come back."

"If you can finish up your work here, I'd be delighted to ask the questions over a bit of dinner, if that's all right with you."

Her smile lit up the place. "Yes, I would enjoy that. It'll take me about a minute and a half."

They were the last ones out of the bank. The guard signed them out, and then he, too, left making sure all the doors were locked up tight.

"We have good roundsmen here in St. Louis," he told McCoy. "Not hardly any trouble with nighttime pranksters or robbers. Fact, we've never been robbed, but keep your elbows crossed so we don't."

McCoy took her to a small nearby restaurant run by some Italian immigrants whose style of cooking had caught his taste buds by surprise more than once. They settled at a table for two toward the back of the eatery, and she put her hands under her chin and watched him.

"You really don't have any questions for me, do you Mr. McCoy?"

"Of course I do. I already asked you one. Now for the second question, what's your first name, or do I have to go on calling you Miss Cloud?"

She laughed, and it brought a smile to his face.

"My parents named me Feather, but when my mother died, Daddy insisted that I have more of

a white name, so we decided on Esther. That's a
Persian name that means star. Also it's Biblical. It's
the Persian name of the captive Hadassahk, whom
Ahesuerus made his queen."

"Your mother was Sioux?"

"No, she was half Osage. My father is all white."

"Your parents created a beautiful combination in
you," he said.

"Thank you. I'm not used to compliments. Some
people don't like it when they find out that I'm part
Indian."

"That's a stupid problem that is entirely their fault.
As for me, I'm fascinated. Will it be all right to call you
Feather?"

For a moment she was quiet, her face showing surprise, then she smiled. "That would please me. May I
call you Spur?"

"That would please me."

When the waiter came McCoy ordered for both of
them. There were three dishes, all with a lot of meat
and cheese and spices. Feather said she had never
tasted anything like it in her life.

They had small cakes in a sauce for dessert, and when
the candle flickered on the table, McCoy realized that
they had spent two hours in the restaurant. The waiter
hovered. McCoy paid the bill, and they walked out into
the early evening.

"I'll see you home," he said.

"Not necessary. I don't live far away."

"I want to see that you get home safely."

She nodded, and they strolled down the dark street.
They had talked of everything during their meal.

McCoy was strangely moved. He'd told this sweet young girl things about his youth he had never told anyone. In response she had shared with him things that had happened to her family and her before they had come here.

He was moved and mystified. How had this happened? She was only another woman. She did not hold his hand nor catch his arm. They walked along together, yet separately. Spur McCoy grinned in the darkness.

In two hours Feather Cloud had become a special friend. He knew that he would never touch her, except perhaps a good night handshake. She was one of those women he met from time to time, maybe once every five years. He knew that here was a woman he could settle down with, who he could spend the rest of his life getting to know and understand and love.

He also knew that it would not happen. He wasn't ready. Hell, he might never be ready. She said something, and he turned toward her.

"Excuse me, Feather, I missed what you said."

"I was only remarking that I've never seen the moon so huge. It looks twice as big here as it does out on the plains or on the coast. Do you think men will ever get to the moon?"

McCoy chuckled. "Doubt if we'll find a bird that big to carry a man all that way. Men have tried to fly for centuries. One over in Europe somewhere glued feathers on his arms and jumped off a high place flapping like crazy. Killed himself. I reckon we'll just have to wait a while until somebody figures out how we can fly.

"What about balloons? Men fly in them."

"True. I saw one once. First one I ever heard of was back in 1830 by a man named Charles Durant in New York City. Went all the way across the Hudson River to New Jersey."

"Some day I want to fly in a balloon," Feather said.

"I hope you do." McCoy shook his head at the glowing orb above them. "That full moon sure can do strange things to people. I haven't thought about that balloon flight for ten years."

They came to her place, an apartment on the second floor of a big building. At the door she turned and held out her hand.

"Mr. Spur McCoy, I thank you for the delightful dinner and the talk. I haven't talked that way for years. I wish you good fortune in finding that counterfeiter. Now I must go up. Father will be worried about me."

He shook her hand.

"Miss Feather Cloud, I have been delighted myself with this evening. I'll remember it for a long time. Perhaps I'll see you again."

She smiled in the half-darkness of the glowing gas lamp on the porch. "Perhaps, Mr. McCoy, but probably not. Good night."

She went through the door, and McCoy turned and walked away. Tonight he would stay in his room at the hotel and wonder what might have been.

Chapter Eight

Agent Jessica Flanders stared at the six-gun almost touching her stomach.

"Mr. Jarek, I want you to consider carefully what you're doing. You are committing assault and battery against me, and you are threatening my life with a firearm. If you move me one foot from where I stand, you will be subject to kidnapping charges. All of these counts could put you in state prison for the rest of your natural life."

"Yeah, yeah, I've heard you lawyers talk before. Just come with us and I won't have to shoot you."

"Have you ever shot a person before, Mr. Jarek?"

He frowned, and he pushed the muzzle against her stomach. "Not as such. Shot at a robber once, but I missed him. I ain't about to miss this close. Now just come around the corner of this building and down the alley a ways. We got somebody mighty anxious to meet you."

"Do you know who I am?"

"Don't know, don't care," the woman beside Jarek said. "Know you're here to cause us a powerful batch of trouble, and we don't aim to see that happen."

"I didn't catch your name, Madam."

"I didn't throw it. Fact is I'm Nan Lattimer, case it'll do you a pea picking batch of good. This misbegotten gent is my brother. You best come along now. He ain't got a whole lot of patience left in him."

The gun jabbed harder now, and Jessica decided to hold her identity secret for a while longer. She'd see what they had in mind for the moment. She turned, with both of them close behind her, walked along the front of the former bank building, turned into the alley and went down it about 30 feet.

Nan Lattimer hurried ahead and opened a door at the back of what Jessica still figured was a bank. She stepped inside and saw two lamps glowing in a dim room without windows.

"Who the hell's there? Who the hell's disturbing me at my work?" The angry bellow came from somewhere ahead.

Jessica's eyes adjusted to the gloom, and soon she saw a towering hulk of a figure bent over some kind of machinery.

"Not to worry, Ed. Just me and some friends."

"Jarek, damn your eyes! Never sneak up on me again that way. Had my blunderbuss out here and half-trigger pulled." The figure had not turned around but simply went on working over the machine that Jessica now saw was a printing press. On a table nearby she spotted dozens of pieces of paper slightly larger than a bank note.

They looked about seven by three inches, the same size as the federal bank notes and silver certificates.

As the trio moved forward slowly, the figure turned around. He wore a dark cape that had a hood on it, so she couldn't really see his face now that his back was to the light.

"Ed, got a new friend for you here. Don't know her name, but she's a pretty little thing. She was getting nosy about the bank."

A roaring bellow of disapproval gushed from the man, and Jessica took a step backward, bumping into Nan Lattimer who snorted.

"What are you doing here in the bank, Ed?" Jessica asked. She knew what he was doing; she wondered if he did.

"Printing. I'm the best damn printer in the state of Missouri."

"What are you printing?"

"Fancy bank notes for the Jefferson City Bank."

"Is that a good thing to do, Ed?"

The hood fell back from his head, and she saw his face from a side lamp. It was scarred and hairless, disfigured so badly it was hard to determine where his features were.

A gaping hole opened again, and he spoke normally.

"Uh, good to print? Yeah, I print all the time. Not much left for me to do. My other press got burned up in the . . . the mess."

"Was it a fire, Ed?"

He flew at her with surprising speed. She had no idea how old he was. The charge lasted only two steps before he faltered, out of breath and out of energy. He stumbled, and only Jarek's rush forward to catch him stopped him from falling.

"Don't . . . never . . . not a good word. Ed don't like it," the hulking figure snarled. He turned then, and the robe fell off his back and dropped down from his arms. The flames had seared all of his torso and his upper arms. Scar tissue showed a deep flame red. He growled and pulled up the robe, fitting it over his head. Jessica saw that either his forearms and hands had not been touched by the fire or the burns had healed naturally.

"What do you do with the bills you print, Ed?" Jessica asked in a pleasant, soft voice.

She was sure he heard her, but he only stood at the press and shook his head.

Nan Lattimer went to the workbench and brought back some of the printed material. In the lamplight she showed the bills to Jessica. These were on oversized paper and still needed to be cut and trimmed to the correct length and width.

"This is professional work, Ed," Jessica said. "Did you make the engraving plates as well?"

His only response was a nod.

Jarek touched Jessica's shoulders, and they moved away from the hulking man toward a small room that had a table, three chairs and a bed which was rumpled and unmade. A small wood burning stove with a smoke pipe out through the wall stood against the brick interior.

Jarek no longer held the gun. He let Jessica and Nan sit down, then he poured them hot coffee from a pot on the stove.

"Now, I ask you, Miss, what else could we do? This is his life. He's a printer. For years he worked on those plates, making them just like the ones they had in Kansas City and over in Nebraska. He was a real printer then, a damn good one. Provided all the work here in town and in three or four other spots along the rail line."

"Then the fire hit his print shop," Nan said taking over the story. "He tried to save it. Jarek and two others had to pull him out of it just before the roof crashed in. Might have been better to leave him there. Took him more than two years to heal. We tried everything we knew. Kept him in a tub of cool water most of the time. It kept him from screaming. Now he's healed, but his mind wanders. How old do you guess he might be?"

Jessica shook her head.

"He was eighty-two last November. Everyone in town takes turns caring for him, bringing in his meals. He lives in this building. Sun hurts his eyes, so he seldom goes outside."

"So what he's really printing is play money?" Jessica said.

"Absolutely. Until about six months ago when some young no goods broke into the bank one night and stole about a gunnysack full of the notes. They're the ones who have been doing the damage. They spent those fives and tens from here to Chicago. Most folks accepted them, 'cause they are printed so well. Most folks don't know towns and banks can't print their own bills anymore like they did back in the late fifties.

"Right after all them bills got stolen was when we scraped the name of the Jefferson City Bank off the front of the window. Didn't want no more bank robbers. Ain't heard nothing from nobody until you showed up."

"Now you've got to stop him," Jessica said. "You'll have to gather up all of those worthless bills and burn them."

Jarek snorted. "Hell, woman, we can't do that. Just suggesting it to Ed would kill him. You want to kill that poor old man?"

"More than ten thousand dollars worth of these bills have shown up at banks across Missouri, Kansas and Illinois. People are going bankrupt when they are proved worthless. One man killed himself when he was ruined. You've got to stop this."

"Just who are you to be ordering us around, Missie?" Nan demanded.

Jessica slowly reached in her reticule and brought out her badge and her identification.

"I'm from Washington and the United States Secret Service. One of our jobs is to stop counterfeiting. Technically that's what Ed is doing here. I could arrest him and both of you and everyone in town who knows about it."

Jarek had his six-gun out again. "No, ma'am, don't reckon we can let you do that. See, Ed is my granddad, and I can't let you or any other federal lawman come in here and do harm to my kin."

"That gun won't stop it from happening. There's a better way. Just change the plates; let him print something else. We can distract him, or maybe when he sleeps, change the plates and destroy the ones that make the bills and put something else in the press. Wouldn't there be a good chance that he wouldn't even notice?"

Nan Lattimer laughed and shook her head. "Not Gramps. He's too sharp for that. The fire didn't hurt one of his eyes. He sees good as ever out of it."

Jarek motioned with the gun. "Sorry, Miss Flanders, but I guess you're going to have to spend the next few days with us until we figure out some way to get Granddad moved to some other small town. We can't have him hurt none, no sir. He's kin, my granddad, and you ain't gonna hurt him."

Jessica looked at the revolver and saw the hammer was cocked. She wouldn't have a chance drawing her own weapon. She put her identification back in her reticule and shrugged as if giving up. Jessica closed the handbag and held it by the foot-long strings. She stood when Jarek motioned for her to do so and turned slightly away from him.

Then she spun back, her reticule with the heavy .38 in it slamming forward toward Jarek's own six-gun like a ten pound hammer.

Spur McCoy found it hard to believe. It was the following morning after he'd walked Feather Cloud home, and now he stared at Priscilla.

"You mean there isn't a single message from Jessica Flanders? Nothing in response to your wire of yesterday morning?"

"Not a thing, Mr. McCoy. I walked past the telegraph office on my way to work this morning. They said the message went out yesterday morning, but there is no record of any reply from Jefferson City."

McCoy made up his mind fast as he always did. "When's the next train west? I've missed the eight-oh-five. Is there one at nine? It's eight-thirty now. I can make a nine o'clock."

Priscilla checked the train schedule. "Yes, nine-ten, westbound. It's a combination train, freight and passengers, so it'll stop at every place along the way. Gets in at Jefferson City a little after noon."

"I'm on it." He gathered up his hat and took two long steps to the connecting door. "I'll take a small bag with my spare weapon and a change of clothes. I hope there's nothing wrong out there in Jefferson City."

Slightly before noon, 80 miles to the west of St. Louis, Secret Service Agent Spur McCoy stepped down from the train at the Jefferson City Station. They had missed three flag stops and two mail stops because no bags were out to be picked up.

He stared down the one-street town. It looked about as he had figured it would—mostly farming and a little ranching this far west in Missouri. He headed for the biggest store in town, the General Store, and had just stepped inside when a thin, rangy man came up to him.

"Just off the train I see. What can I do for you this morning?"

"Like some cigars, two for a nickel if'n you have any."

"Certainly. One of my most popular items among smokers. How many today?"

"A dozen."

McCoy paid for the cheroots, put eleven of them in his shirt pocket and lit the other one. Then he lifted his small carpetbag and left the store. The man was not friendly, but not hostile either.

The agent took a slow walk down one side of the main street and up the other. One building in the middle of town looked like it could have been a bank, but the front window was washed clean and then probably whitewashed from the inside. There were no letters of any kind showing through the whiteness. Still it could have been a bank at one time.

No other building in town remotely resembled the rock solid edifice that a financial institution should be, nor was there any structure that claimed to be a bank now or that had once been one.

He saw only two saloons, not many for a town of this size. Must be a stay-at-home, churchgoing crowd. He tried the larger of the two and stepped through the door into a dark, smoky interior.

He went to the bar and asked for a beer.

"Warm all right? Our ice house ran dry last month."

"Set a case or two outside come sundown and it'll stay chilled all day."

The barkeep was probably also the owner. Only two other men in the place worked on mugs of beer, and he could see no girls. Figured. He accepted the warm mug of suds and tossed the barkeep a dime. He got half that back in change.

"Lively looking little town," McCoy said. "I just got off the noon train out of St. Louis."

The barkeep nodded and wiped the clean mahogany again.

"You here selling?" he asked.

McCoy knew it was a shot in the dark. He wasn't dressed in the white shirt and dark suit that was the trademark of the drummer.

"No, thankfully. Just looking around with the idea of setting up a business. Anything this town needs? How about a good bordello with about six girls out of Chicago?"

The barkeep snorted. "City council ran the last of the whores out of town ten years ago. Not about to get any more set up here. Them five old men come down hard on anything they don't like. Damn tough for me to make a living here with no tits around, but I manage."

"Town fathers that tough?"

"Damn site tougher—straight and Baptist most of them. Me and Old Ben got the only saloons in town and they keep rooting at us, but we got the damn U.S. Constitution backing us up and we're staying in business."

"Yeah, it's a free country."

"Damn right."

"One thing bothers me. Somebody said there wasn't no bank in town. Mean I'd have to get on the train and go down the tracks to the county seat for some banking services?"

"About the size of it. Had a bank here ten, twelve years ago, but it went bust. Roiled a bunch of good folks. Now most everyone banks for hisself. Oh, there is Mr. Jarek who owns the General Store. He does some lending at interest now and again."

"But not a business loan or a line of credit, I'd imagine," McCoy said.

"You got that right."

"Think a hardware store would go here?"

"Get most of that kind of goods from the General Store."

"But I'd carry a lot of things he can't. All sorts of hinges and maybe roofing and even some lumber."

"Might work. Might not. Tougher in this town. Half the folks here are related."

"You're talking me into getting back on the train."

"Might be the best move you made all day. We got another westbound long about three o'clock."

McCoy finished his beer, waved his thanks and strode out the door. A scattering of clouds shaded the sun.

He moved down to the hotel, a two-story affair. Inside it was clean enough. A middle-aged woman smiled at him from behind the desk.

"You been looking over our town, so what do you think? Nice clean community, church-minded, plenty of business. You looking to settle or to go into business?"

"Maybe a little of both. Figure first I'll get a room and rest up a little. You have one left?"

"Matter-of-fact, I do." She turned a register book around to him, and he dipped the pen in the ink bottle and scratched down his moniker. He scanned the rest of the page and saw that Jessica's name was not on that sheet. Some entry two lines above his had been marked out completely so it couldn't be read.

He flipped the book around.

"Say I was scouting for a new business. What about law and order? A town marshal, sheriff, policeman? What do we have here?"

"Not much of any right now. Sheriff called the deputy back since he had nothing to do here. We take care of ourselves just fine. Anything happen we wire the sheriff and he comes in."

"I hear the old bank is closed up. How would I get change, cash checks, have an account to pay my bills if I was running a business? What do you do?"

"Mostly cash here. I manage to keep enough change around. Not a real problem. The merchants help each other out. They got two banks over in the county seat about twenty-five miles west."

"Oh, then it sounds like I couldn't run to the bank every morning."

"Not likely. You're in room eight. That's ground floor and to the right down there that-a-way."

"Thanks for your help. I may want to talk some new business ideas with you later on."

"Always use new money in a town this size."

He found the room which was sparse, clean and simple with a bed, chair, wash bowl and pitcher of water on a small stand. He tried the bed. Better than sleeping on the ground, but not much.

McCoy stood behind the thin white curtains and stared out the window. It opened on the front of the hotel and looked across the street at the building he thought once could have been the bank.

As he watched he saw a man turn down the alley beside the building, pause, look around a moment, then vanish into a door of the old bank building. Interesting.

It was a place to start, but not until after dark. He made up his mind quickly. Jarek, the General Store, was the rich man in town. If there was any counterfeiting here, he'd know about it. Telling might be a different thing.

Spur left his bag under the bed and made certain that a small string linked through the two handles. If anyone opened it, they wouldn't see the string which would be on the floor when he returned.

He adjusted his six-gun on his hip and left the hotel with a wave to the owner. McCoy made no wasted moves. He marched directly to the General Store and entered. Jarek had just finished waiting on someone. The customer looked at McCoy curiously and then left by the front door.

"Ah, yes, the cheroot man. Smoked those twelve up already?"

"No, I'm a United States Secret Serviceman here to inspect the Jefferson City Bank. You know about it, and you know what happened to Agent Jessica Flanders." McCoy drew his Peacemaker .45 Colt and held the muzzle toward the floor.

"You have about thirty seconds to start talking, then I'm putting handcuffs on you and taking you back to St. Louis with me. Now, where is Jessica and where is the damned Jefferson City Bank?"

Chapter Nine

Hirum Jarek stared at the six-gun and the handcuffs that Agent McCoy had just pulled from his pocket as he threatened to arrest the store owner. His eyes bulged for a moment, and his hands came up in denial.

"Now hold on there, Agent McCoy, or whoever you are. We got laws in this country, and they don't allow anyone running around with a fancy title and a gun and then stomping all over us. Fact is, I don't know nothing of what you're talking about. There is no Jefferson City Bank."

McCoy pulled one of the spurious Jefferson City Bank $5 notes from his pocket and pushed in front of Jarek's face.

"You can see, can't you? You can read. It says the Jefferson City Bank of Jefferson City, Missouri. A note payable in gold by the Jefferson City Bank."

"I've never seen that note before in my life," Jarek said. McCoy spun him around, whipped his hands behind his long, lean body and fastened the cuffs on him. Then he grabbed his shoulder and marched the man toward the front door.

"No, not a step farther!" A woman's voice rang out from the rear of the store. McCoy stopped, looked back and saw the twin barrels of a Greener aimed over the counter near the cash drawer. He could see only the top of a gray-haired head on the other side of the counter.

"Lay down your weapon, Mr. Lawman, and then take them infernal manacles off my brother."

McCoy spun around, grabbed Jarek and pulled him in front of his body, facing the shotgun.

"Don't reckon you'll gun down your own kin to get at me, whoever you are. Stand up and put your hands on top of your head or I'm going to start putting slugs through that thin counter front and punch some nasty, bloody holes in your body."

"Oh, dear." The woman's head vanished for a moment, then a hand pushed the shotgun out of reach on top of the counter. Slowly the woman stood up. She looked to be in her early forties, dressed plain and proper.

"Your name, please," McCoy said, his Peacemaker still covering her.

"Nan Standish," the woman said. "Don't hurt my brother."

"We won't hurt him. He'll have a nice comfortable jail cell in St. Louis, probably all to himself. Judge probably will send him to prison for a year and a day."

"Oh, no, not that!" the woman wailed.

"Then suppose you tell me about the Jefferson City Bank and where Miss Jessica Flanders is."

"Well, about the bank. Never was one really. Our grandfather—we call him Gramps—used to have this print shop." She told him about the fire, the innocent printing of the fake play money, and the robbery.

"So it ain't our fault 'tall. Some robbing owlhoot stole them bills thinking they were real."

"Over ten thousand dollars worth are in circulation," McCoy said. "When banks get them, they refuse to honor them and send them to us. More than one small business has gone bankrupt because of your grandfather's little game. Now where is Agent Jessica Flanders?"

"She's at my place in a locked room," Mrs. Standish said. "No chance she can get out. I'll trade you her for leaving Gramps alone."

"Not a chance, Mrs. Standish. Right now you take me to Jessica, or I'm going to arrest your brother and charge him with counterfeiting."

"Oh, dear, it wasn't supposed to happen this way."

"It never is. Do you want to see Jarek here in jail, or will you take me to Miss Flanders?"

"I'll lock the front door and then take you to my place out the back. Reckon Jarek will have to come, too."

"I reckon."

Five minutes later McCoy pushed Jarek, still cuffed, through the front door of his sister's modest two-story house. It was only a block off Main Street. They went up the stairs, and the woman nodded at a door at the end of the hall.

"It was a small room for storage. No windows but plenty of light. I even put a mattress on the floor for her to sleep on."

"Thoughtful of you. Now open the door." McCoy raised his voice. "Jessica, if you're in there don't do anything rash. Everything is under control."

Mrs. Standish opened a half-inch steel bolt and pushed the door inward. Jessica stood in the middle of the room waiting for them. She was fully dressed and held her reticule in one hand, the small brown hat in the other.

"About time you got here, McCoy. Make Jarek give me back my .38, then I'll show you the counterfeiting setup."

McCoy chuckled. "You're welcome for your thanks for my rescuing you. You all right?"

"Only a slight bruise on my shoulder. I got it when I knocked Jarek's gun away with my purse and he tackled me. They tell you about the crazy old man?"

"He is not crazy," Mrs. Standish said. "He just needs a little care. After all, he's eighty-two now."

It was ten minutes later before Jessica had her .38 revolver back in her purse and she led the four of them to the side door of the old bank building. Jarek was still in handcuffs, and several of the locals stared at the strange scene.

"They set it up right in here," Jessica said. "Even humored the old man by painting the name on the window saying Jefferson City Bank." She pushed open the alley door and stepped into the dark interior.

McCoy struck a kitchen match and looked around. He spotted an oil lamp on a big wooden box and lit the wick, then put the glass chimney back in place.

"Before the press was right over here," Jessica said.

The entire room was bare except for the one wooden box.

"They moved him," Jessica said. "Mrs. Standish there said that's what they would have to do. First I need to find just one of those bills in this room to prove that the printing was done here."

Jarek laughed. "Kind of hard to prove who did the printing, ain't it, McCoy? You best undo my cuffs here before I bring an unjust arrest charge against you."

"You're just in custody, not under arrest, Jarek. You've got no case. You might have when I formally arrest you and take you east on the next train. What time does it leave?"

"Four-thirty," Mrs. Standish replied without thinking. Then she frowned, berating herself silently.

"Good," McCoy said. "That gives us a few more minutes for one of you to tell us where Gramps and his printing press are. Otherwise, Jarek here goes in handcuffs, under arrest, all the way back to St. Louis."

Mrs. Standish crossed her arms over her ample chest and scowled. "Leastwise the government will have to buy his ticket. He'll enjoy seeing the big town. He's never been there. Besides, you don't got no charges that's gonna stick.

"I sure do," Jessica said. "Pointing a weapon at a federal officer, assault and battery, kidnapping . . ."

"Just who do you have for witnesses to all of those terrible crimes?" Mrs. Standish asked.

"You were there, Mrs. Standish. I'll call you as a witness."

"I never seen nothing. Fact is, I was in my dress shop all that afternoon."

McCoy cleared his throat. "Afraid what the lady says is right, Jessica. We don't have enough witnesses. But then neither do they. Why don't you take Mrs. Standish outside for about five minutes, and I'll see how much persuasion I can use on Mr. Jarek here. He doesn't look like he can stand pain too well. Mr. Jarek, have you ever had both of your thumbs broken at the same time?"

Jarek began to edge away from McCoy and shook his head.

"No cause to get violent here," Jarek said. "We made a deal. You get the girl back, and you don't fool with Gramps."

"That was *your* deal. I never agreed to it. Now Jessica, you just hustle that little gray-haired lady into the alley. You can leave the alley door open in case she wants to listen to her kin in here taking some punishment."

"Right, McCoy. I can do that." She grabbed Mrs. Standish and propelled her towards the alley door. They were almost there when Mrs. Standish stopped.

"No, don't hurt him. Fact is, he don't know where Gramps is. Me and three lady friends moved him last night."

"Is he at your house?"

"No, he won't stay with me. Tried to get him to stay there time and again."

"Let's see," McCoy said. "Jarek, I'd figure that you should take in forty, maybe fifty dollars a day at your store. With you in custody for, say two weeks before a judge releases you in St. Louis—that would mean you could be out as much as seven hundred dollars. Sounds like one pile of money to me. You have a spare seven hundred to throw away like that?"

Jarek shook his head. "You know I don't, McCoy. You also know that Gramps ain't no criminal. It can't be a crime to print fake money if you don't spend any of it. I bet any fair judge would say that Gramps is not guilty of anything but bad luck, that damn fire, and some owlhoots who did the passing of the play money. The man is eighty-two years old, for God's sake."

McCoy took another tactic. "Let's say, just for the sake of argument, that your Grandfather is not guilty of passing any money. Printing it is also a crime, but we could show that he had no intent to pass the bills. I'm sure that would go well with any judge in the land. Then, knowing his physical and emotional condition, I'm sure the judge would be lenient. So instead of all that trouble, why don't we settle this right here and now without the help of a federal judge or a trip to St. Louis."

"Now you're talking more sense," Jarek said. "What kind of a bargain can we arrange here? We already gave you back the lady agent."

"That's something else we'll have to talk about. First, Gramps. You've moved him somewhere here in town. The way half the town is interrelated, you could probably go on moving him every day or so for a year and we'd never find him. We don't have the time for that."

"We'll promise that no more of the fake bills will ever get outside of the room where he's working," Mrs. Standish said.

"Not good enough," McCoy countered. "I have to go back to my boss with those plates."

"He worked ten years on those plates as an engraver," Jarek said. "They are his pride and his life. Without them he'd wither up and die in a week."

"Then let's have him do some more engraving," McCoy said. He held up one of the five dollar bills. "See this big circle in red on the left. Across it in quarter inch letters, I want him to engrave at an angle: PLAY MONEY. Then below that: NOT NEGOTIABLE."

"He'll know what that means," Mrs. Standish said.

"He also knows about the robbers," McCoy said. "All you have to do is convince him that he must do this. Then he can print all the money that he wants to, and he might even be able to sell it to a game company."

Jarek nodded slowly. "Yes, it might work. He has three sets of plates, the ones, fives and tens. He'd have to engrave on all of them. That would keep him busy for two months."

"What else?" Mrs. Standish asked.

"We'll have to gather up all of the printed bills, save a few representative ones, then burn everything else," Jessica said.

Mrs. Standish took a deep breath and then sighed. "I guess we can convince him that we're sending the money to a bank that wants it. He won't like it, but then he'll have to print up some more of the new bills with the play money words across them."

McCoy reached over and tapped Jarek on the shoulder. "Does this sound possible to you, Mr. Jarek?"

He nodded. "Yes, but it'll take some doing, probably the rest of today and tonight. We'll give you our answer first thing in the morning."

McCoy looked at Jessica. "That sound reasonable to you, Jess?"

She said it did. "I'll go wire a report to Pris and to the general."

McCoy took the handcuffs off Jarek's wrists. "Looks like we have a deal. I'll print up on a bill the size of the letters and the spelling so there's no mistake. I want it black ink on the red, so it will stand out."

"Yes, yes," Jarek said rubbing his wrists. "I used to help him in his print shop years ago. That can be done easily. Now all I have to do is convince him to do as you say."

"Be persuasive. If you can't, we'll have to take some action against him for printing those bills."

Jessica and Spur went to the telegraph office at the small depot and sent the wires.

They had an early dinner at a pleasant cafe and were pleased with the food. Then they headed for the hotel. Jessica's bag was waiting for them.

The woman behind the desk nodded. "Hear you'll be wanting a room, Miss. My sister says you're working with the lawman there, so I'll put you in number seven, right down the hall, first floor."

Jessica said that would be fine and signed the register. When McCoy walked her down to the room, she motioned him inside, then closed the door and locked it.

When she turned around and faced him, Jessica Flanders had a secret smile. She stepped over to

McCoy, reached up and kissed his lips. Then she found his right hand and placed it over her breast. She kissed him again, and a moment later their tongues were fighting each other.

When the hot kiss ended, she smiled even sweeter. "McCoy, I've heard that you're a devil with the women on your cases. Everyone talks about you. Now I think it's time I see if all of those stories and wild rumors are true." She stepped back and began to unbutton the top of her dress, and McCoy grinned right back at her and helped with the buttons.

Chapter Ten

Jennifer caught his hands at her buttons and watched him until he looked down at her.

"Don't you even want to know why?"

"I'm not the curious type, but since I started out being so angry with you, I guess I do want to know why."

"Good." She let him undo the buttons until she could lift the dress off over her head. She wore three petticoats under the dress and a chemise.

He lifted the petticoats off one by one until she had on only the chemise, silk underpants and high white stockings that came halfway up her delightful thighs.

She began working on his clothing then, insisting that she do it all herself. By the time she had his shirt off and his longjohns unbuttoned to show his hairy chest, she told him.

"I promised myself that I had come on too strong with you back in St. Louis. Then when I got caught here in

107

Jefferson City by Jarek, I promised myself that if you ever rescued me, I'd undress and do you proper the way a thankful female should."

"Just gratitude? No desire? This is just a reward for saving your fancy little bottom from being kidnapped and locked up in a stuffy room?"

She pulled the chemise off and let him stare at her breasts. They were fuller than he had imagined, with rosebuds for nipples and wide pink areolas that seemed to darken even as he watched them.

He bent and kissed each breast, heard her quick gasps of pleasure or surprise and looked up at her.

"Mr. McCoy . . ."

"I'd like you to call me Spur, whether we're here in bed fucking up a storm or at the office."

She grinned at the naughty word.

"Don't try to shock me. My father was a cop and a good one and had a vocabulary that could make a longshoreman blush. Fine, I'll call you Spur, and as far as desire goes . . ." She pulled his face down toward her breasts again.

"Desire? I learned about making love when I was seventeen. He was the boy next door, and he never had made love before either, except with the pleasures of his hand. We tore off each other's clothes and romped around in the sunshine and petted and experimented.

"We both had talked to older siblings and knew how it was done, no big secret there, but at first he couldn't get into me. I used some saliva on his penis, and it slid right in. We made love seven times in just a little over an hour. He couldn't get enough, and neither could I."

She moved and eased her other pulsating breast into his mouth. "I was lucky that day that I didn't get pregnant. He came back for more, but I told him never again until I was married, and he ran so fast I thought he had a rocket in his pants.

"I had heard about you and the ladies when I was in Washington D.C. As soon as I checked in with Priscilla, I asked her if the rumors were anywhere near true, and she told me yes but that she had never even seen your body with your shirt off, let alone made love to you."

He lifted himself off of her breasts, slid out of his boots, pants and longjohns, then hooked his thumbs in the silk underpants she wore. Her hands caught his.

"In a moment. You talked about desire, about passion. I really need to get warmed up a little more first."

He picked her up, kissed her and eased her down gently on the bed. Her eyes came open, and he slipped down beside her, his hands working on her breasts. He left her lips and kissed her cheek, then pushed back her dark short hair and licked her ear.

"Oh, glory!" she whispered. He licked it again, and she caught him with her arms and held him tightly.

"That . . . that is so delightfully sexy!"

He licked the crook of her neck under her chin, and her hands moved to find his crotch and found him only half-aroused. She looked at him in surprise.

"Don't I excite you? You aren't even hard yet."

"Sometimes I need a little warming up as well."

"Oh, Lord! I was thinking only of myself." She sat up, pushed him down and fondled his balls and limp penis. She bent down and kissed the soft head, and McCoy felt a surge of desire.

She laughed softly. "He likes that."

"Most do," McCoy said. He got his hands back on her breasts and kneaded and petted them. He could feel her nipples harden and flush with hot blood. She kissed his manhood again and licked it until it was fully erect.

She caught his hands as she lay beside him and moved them to her underpants. "Please now, Spur, take them off and touch me down there. I'm getting so hot I want to scream."

He pulled down the soft garment and tossed it to the floor. Slowly she spread her legs. His hand came up her leg gently, petting, caressing, warming the inside of her thigh. Her breathing came faster now. She opened her eyes and watched him. His finger circled the damp spot at her crotch, and she cried out in excitement. Then he brushed his hand across her small hard node and she gasped. He set up a rhythm, rubbing the node back and forth, playing it like a banjo.

"Oh, God!" she whispered, then her hips bounced upwards and her whole body shook in a grinding, climax that made her gasp and cry out in delight. When the last of the spasms had torn through her, Jessica opened her eyes in amazement.

"Nobody in the world ever did that for me before," she said, her eyes wide, her breath still coming in gasps. "Lordy, but that was fine, just ever so fine."

She pulled him over her then, and he found her slot. Though it was wet with her own juices, he added some of his own, then looked down at her.

"You sure this is all right with you, Jess?"

"Dear Lord, yes. Now hurry or I know that I'll just burst."

He slid into her, and she sighed and then yelped in delight, her small hips pounding upward to gain as much penetration as possible.

"Oh!" she cried out in sudden pain. "You . . . you touched something in there that nobody's ever even come close to before. You must be so big!"

He eased off a little, then began to stroke slowly all the way in and all the way out until she yelped in wonder and her hips began to buck again.

This time he beat her to it, kicking in fast and hard, slamming into her and nudging her higher and higher on the bed. He pounded seven hard strokes more before he climaxed and eased down on top of her.

Her arms went around his shoulders, and they lay there for five minutes before she let him go. He eased away from her, dropping beside her on his back, his hand reaching to find hers.

"You're two ahead of me," he said.

She smiled at him. "I know. I've never been so sensitive before. I guess it was just wanting you so much and knowing how good you were going to be. I'm glad we had this time. Promise me that you never, ever will tell Pris."

Spur grinned. "I won't have to tell her. She'll look at you when we get back to the office and she'll give me an angry stare and she'll know. Don't ask me how she does it, but she can always tell."

"She wants you, Spur."

"I know, but that would ruin our business relationship. I keep the two strictly separate, then she doesn't get hurt."

Jessica leaned up on one elbow and watched him. "You've never been married?"

"Ours isn't the kind of a job a wife or a husband would understand or put up with. I'm better off this way."

"You don't ever want to settle down?"

"Someday, when I get tired of the field work. The general said he's got a spot for me in Washington working at a desk. Reckon that won't be for a few years yet. Maybe then, I'll find a winsome widow and settle down."

"More likely your bride will be some sexy and shapely sweet young thing half your age, and before you get out of bed, you'll have six kids." They both laughed.

"Again," she said reaching for him.

It was a long but rewarding night. Five times they satisfied each other, the last just before 4:00 A.M. when they drifted off to sleep.

The next morning, they had breakfast at the café across the street and met Jarek at his store shortly after he opened at 8:00 o'clock. The thin, tall man nodded curtly.

"Well, I done it. He didn't want to do it, said it would spoil the new bills, but I promised him they would work just as well. I convinced him at last. Wasn't easy, but I guess it'll be worth it."

"What about the already printed bills?" Jessica asked.

He shot her an angry glance, then sighed. "Hell, I had to buy them from him. He said he'd sell the whole print batch for twenty dollars. I paid him in brand new one dollar federal bank notes so it looked like more. Got all the Jefferson City Bank bills in a cardboard box in back."

"Let's see them," McCoy said.

Jarek led them past a curtain into the storeroom. It was stacked with boxes that almost reached the ceiling. It smelled of old leather and new saddles. Jarek stopped at a carton sitting on a small workbench, opened it and stepped away.

Jessica looked inside and cried out in surprise. "So many of them. How long has he been printing these?"

"Going on two years now. Does a few every day, but they stack up. Most of these aren't cut to size even. He doesn't like to do that. The stolen ones weren't cut either."

"You're sure this is all of them?" Jessica asked.

"Absolutely. My sister moved him to a vacant house near her place so she can help take care of him. She said she picked up every one at the old bank and around his new print shop in one of the bedrooms. They're all here. We find any more I'll promise to burn them soon as I see them."

McCoy nodded. "That's good enough for me. You have a stove back here to keep this place warm in the winter?"

He did, and the two agents took turns tossing handfuls of the spurious Jefferson City Bank paper money into the stove. It took them almost a half hour.

By then, Mrs. Standish had come to the store. Jessica had saved three of each denomination, put them in an envelope and tucked it into her reticule.

Spur McCoy took a pen and a bottle of black ink and printed the word he wanted across the red circle: PLAY MONEY and NOT NEGOTIABLE. He gave the bill to Mrs. Standish.

"Lord, he was upset about adding these words to his engravings. Kept asking me why he needed to put this on them. I told him it was the new banking laws and he had to follow them just as any other bank or he'd get us all in trouble. That convinced him."

"How long will it take him to do the engravings on both sides of the plates for the three bills?" McCoy asked.

"He said about a week. A week means nothing to him. I'll see to it that he does it proper."

Jessica listened and nodded. "Mrs. Standish, as soon as he has the first plate done on both sides, have him print me five of the bills and mail them to me at our St. Louis address. That way we'll be sure that everything is as it should be and we won't have to come back out here. Do that with the next two fake bills as well."

Mrs. Standish gave a sigh and nodded. "Lordy, I'm so thankful this is at last cleared up. Half the town's been holding its breath since them sidewinders stole all them paper money bills from the old bank. Now we can relax a little. Not sure if Gramps knew he was doing anything wrong or not."

"Either way, I think that the Secret Service will be satisfied," McCoy said. He looked at Jessica who seemed to have a small secret smile this morning. "When does the next eastbound train leave?"

Jessica looked at Mrs. Standish.

"There's a train through at a quarter of eleven. If you

hurry, you should be able to catch it."

"I don't think I can be ready in that time," Jessica said. "When's the next one?"

"One-thirty or so," Jarek said.

They shook hands all around, then the two agents headed for the hotel.

"Curious why you didn't think you could be ready to leave on the earlier train," McCoy said.

She grinned at him. "I'll bet you can think of the reason, if you'll really put your mind to it." She caught his arm and pulled it against her so it brushed her breast. "At least I hope you can figure out what we might do for another couple of hours in your hotel room."

He figured it out.

They made the 1:30 train with only half a minute to spare and laughed all the way to their seats. Jessica was still flushed from the power of the last roaring climax in the hotel room just before they dressed and ran for the train.

It was a three and a half hour train ride to St. Louis and they sat close together and talked. By the time they got to St. Louis they both knew most of what was important about each other and a lot that would be of no value at all.

As they got off in St. Louis and hailed a cab, he cautioned her again about Priscilla. "Don't be surprised if she asks you point blank. I've had Pris do it before. Just take it casually, but don't go into any details, for God's sake. I don't want any more trouble with Pris. She's the best helper I've ever had in the office, and I don't want to lose her."

When they walked into the office with their over-night carpetbags, Priscilla jumped up from her desk and ran to meet them. She grinned at McCoy, said the general had replied to his solution to the Jefferson City Bank swindle and agreed with his actions.

She looked at Jessica. "We were so worried about you. Were you in any danger? I want to take you to dinner tonight and have you tell me all about it. I wonder if I could ever be a female agent? You're a person I really respect and look up to."

McCoy went to his desk, looked at the stack of mail and discarded the obviously nonessential items. He read the wire from the general first, then scanned his mail and found nothing that would sidetrack him from the problem of the $20 bill counterfeiter.

He tried to get Priscilla's eye twice, then called out. "Miss Quincy, might I have a word with you?"

She came directly with a notebook and a pencil. "Yes, Mr. McCoy. A letter?"

"No. Anything new on the Flavian Kirby counterfeiting case?"

"Oh, yes, there is something. A note came for you sometime last night from a Mr. Rhodenway. He says our suspect was there but no one found out where he was staying. He said you might contact him at your convenience."

"Damnit, Pris, why didn't you tell me that the second I got in the door?" He grabbed his hat, adjusted his gunbelt and marched out the door.

Chapter Eleven

It was a little after 5:30 when Spur McCoy rang the bell at the Club and waited for the sliding panel to open. Rhodenway saw him and opened the door at once.

"Miss Melissa wants to talk to you. I understand you were out of town for a time." The tall, dignified man motioned, and a pretty young girl came and took McCoy's arm and led him up one flight and down the hall to Melissa's suite. The girl knocked on the door, then opened it and ushered McCoy inside.

Melissa came through a curtain that warded off her office area. She nodded at McCoy and showed him four $20 bills.

"All fakes, all with the number you gave us. We know who the little bastard is, but we kept accepting his money until you got here. Where the hell were you last night?"

McCoy explained, and she was somewhat mollified.

"The little man has an appointment for six-thirty for dinner first. This is four nights in a row. I'd guess the old man may only have dinner and a little messing around tonight. His wad is about shot for a week or so."

"Anywhere I can observe him coming and then leaving?"

She led him down the hall to a small room near the front of the building. It had an intricate lattice work front to it, and through the slats he could see most of the entryway and the front door. Rhodenway stood beside the door, stiff and formal, waiting for the next knock or ring.

"Six-thirty, you said. Is he on time?"

"Usually. You know that no one leaves by our front door but uses the side door on Whatley Street. I'd suggest you be there waiting with a buggy. He's latched on to Delphine again. I'll have her walk him to the back door and give you some kind of a signal when he leaves."

The madam of the most expensive parlor in town watched him. "Anything else?"

"That seems to cover it. We won't arrest him here, of course, as we promised. We want to follow him back to wherever he's staying and try to get the plates back."

"Yes. Fine." She looked at him closely. "You want some company up here while you wait? The door locks. It's on the house, of course. Any of the ladies except Delphine. She's getting ready. The little joker demands a freshly bathed girl."

"The man lives well. No one for me tonight, thanks. Not that I don't appreciate the offer, but I better wait alone and tend to business."

"You're a good cop, Spur. Hope you catch the little bastard tonight. I'm tired of fooling around with him."

"We should do it tonight. I need to go out and make some arrangements, but I'll be back here well before six-thirty."

Once outside, McCoy hurried to Jessica's hotel room in the Claymore and knocked.

She came to the door and opened it a crack, with the muzzle of her .38 showing along with a slice of her face.

"Oh, McCoy."

"We've got a lead on Flavian Kirby. Tonight at the Club. I need you to rent a cab and wait by the side door with me so we can tail him when he leaves."

Jessica opened the door and waved him inside. She stood there in her chemise and petticoats.

"See how much easier this is after last night? Wait until I get into a dress and some better shoes, and I'll be ready."

McCoy watched with a touch of sadness as the dress covered up her sleek body, then he remembered it all naked and writhing and humping.

On the street they rented a cab at the livery, then drove to the side entrance to the Club.

"Now, you wait here, and I'll go inside and try to identify him on his way in at six-thirty. Then when he's upstairs, I'll come out here and wait with you. He usually takes one of that line of cabs waiting over there across the street near the side door. A good stand for those cabbies, I've heard."

Jessica shook her pretty head. "What a business! It's just a whorehouse with a bar and a kitchen. Evidently a lot of men go nuts over the place. It must be well furnished."

He told her from what he had seen of it, that it was expensive and in good taste.

"Hey, maybe I should apply for a job. Those girls are living a lot fancier than I am."

"They also work harder. Most of them are on a half hour schedule, unless it's an all-nighter."

She looked at him curiously and grinned. "You ever had an all-nighter at a whorehouse?"

"Never paid for making love in my life."

"That's not answering the question."

He laughed softly. "I've had a few good friends who just happened to be fancy ladies, and they invited me to spend the night. But no money changed hands."

"Ah hah!" Jessica said.

He stepped out of the cab, then walked around the block to the front door of the Club.

One minute before 6:30, Flavian Kirby, going by the name of Mr. Amway, stepped into the entryway of the Club, was greeted formally by Rhodenway and had a young girl escort him down the hallway and out of sight. McCoy wondered where the money changed hands— perhaps with the escorts to the room or maybe with the whores themselves. He went down the stairs and out the side door.

That way no one going out saw anyone coming in. It was all extremely private without even a central dining room. He waved away a cabby who hurried forward and walked down a block until he came to the buggy they had rented.

Jessica sat in the rig with one hand in her reticule, gripping her .38. She had brought a jacket which was tucked around her to ward off the October night breeze. She made room for McCoy to step into the rig.

"We have our quarry in the nest. Now when he comes out, we'll be ready."

"How long? Half the night?"

"No, this is his fourth night in a row, Miss Melissa said. She guessed it would be dinner and a little messing around and that he would pull out before eight o'clock."

"Let's hope so," Jessica said. "I'm cold and I'm hungry and I was wishing that we were up in my hotel room tearing our clothes off."

McCoy put his arm around her and drew her close. "I can help you stay a little warmer." His left hand slid under her jacket, worked through two buttons, then closed around one of her trembling breasts.

"Oh, glory! You do know how to warm up a girl. That feels ever so much better."

"Nothing serious here," he said kissing her cheek. "Just a little warming up for a lovely lady."

She snuggled against him and sighed. "Oh, yes, now this is what detective work should be all about. If we have to wait for someone, we can at least be comfortable." Jessica grinned, reached up and kissed his lips. Then she settled down against him.

More than a dozen men came out the well-lighted side door and hailed cabs. None of them was short enough to be their target. By 8:00 o'clock they wondered aloud if Miss Melissa had misjudged her customer.

"He could have more sexual stamina that we figured," Morgan said softly. Jessica sighed and moved his hand from one breast to the other.

"Another candidate," McCoy said. A woman stood momentarily in the doorway and waved—Delphine, the signal. "Yes, he's the right size, and he has that silly black derby hat on tonight. He wore it when he came. Not a lot of them around this town. And that's Delphine making sure we know that's him." McCoy retrieved his hand from her breast and both sat up straighter. Their rig was pointing the same way as the hacks across the street. They watched Kirby take the second hack in line. It swung out and rolled down the street.

In the gloom of the pale moon and only an occasional gas street lamp, McCoy followed the hack half a block behind. He held back when the small man got out of the rig in front of the Mayflower Hotel.

"This is a natural place for him to stay. Expensive, elegant and exclusive." He parked three doors down at the curb and walked along the concrete sidewalk with Jessica.

"Trying to figure out how to handle this. The hotel has a doorman. Might even be hard to get in without showing our badges, but we don't want to tip him off. I'll show my badge as a last resort."

He had to. The doorman didn't know their names, had never heard of a Mr. Amyway or a Mr. Kirby and wouldn't let them inside until they showed their badges.

At the desk McCoy took a harder attitude.

"A man just came in here two minutes ago. He has called himself Mr. Amway. You saw him. How is he registered and what's his room number?"

"I'm sorry, but I can't give out—"

"You'll tell me now, or I'll put handcuffs on you and

arrest you for interfering with a law officer. Which will it be?"

The clerk was older than McCoy and knew how the police and lawmen could operate. He nodded and handed a small card to McCoy.

It listed the man in room 303 as J.A. Archibald, formerly of New York City, in town on a vacation.

McCoy gave the card back. "Don't warn him in any way that we're on our way to see him, or you'll really get in trouble."

The clerk nodded, and McCoy and Jessica hurried to the stairs and up to room 303. They stood on each side of the door as McCoy knocked three times. Nothing happened. McCoy knocked again, but no one answered the door.

McCoy fumbled in his pocket and came up with a ring of skeleton keys. The fourth key he tried worked, and he edged the door open.

Down the hall at room 308, the door silently opened a narrow crack and a solitary eye watched the pair at room 303. The man watching smiled, then scowled. Someone was after him. Somehow he had been identified. Perhaps at that damn Club. He'd spent enough of the counterfeit bills there.

His mind whirled. What to do now? He had left a valise, clothes and personal items in the room so it would look occupied. He had even rumpled the bed to make it look as if he had taken an afternoon nap. But none of the money was in the room nor any identification.

What next? They would watch the room and wait for him to come back. Evidently they had followed him from the Club and browbeat the room clerk for his room number. The clerk knew nothing about 308. He had bribed one of the bellboys to mark the room occupied under another name and even enter room payments.

Now he had to get out of this hotel, out of St. Louis. Damnit, Delphine! He knew he was spending too much time with her. She had been the best woman he had ever known or fucked. Damnit! Now where would he go? He had plenty of good money left. It was hard to spend more than one of the brand new bills at a time. He had crumpled them and spilled sand and dirt over them to make them look worn, but some clerks had sharp eyes.

He continued to watch room 303. It took them just five minutes to search the room, then ease out the door. A man and a woman? Must be federal lawmen. He wasn't worried about them, but they were a complication. He had taken the precaution of getting this room that opened on a fire escape that ran down the side of the building.

Then what? The bellboy he bribed to get this room was off duty now. They would have no way of checking which room he was in except by a room to room search, and the management here wouldn't allow that. He had enough money, but he needed to pass some more and get change. St. Louis was getting too hot for him. He had to move on. A boat! He'd grab a river boat and go downstream. New Orleans!

Quickly he gathered up all his belongings. He heard noises in the hall and watched again as the two detectives came out of his room, each walking to opposite ends of the hallway. By the time the woman came to his door he had eased it fully closed. She passed, and he breathed easier.

It took him another five minutes to pack the rest of his clothes and goods in his big traveling bag. The smaller valise held the plates and a stack of blank paper as well as his store of $88,000 in $20 bills. He could afford to drop the heavy bag but never the valise.

He waited another half hour, then checked the hall but could spot neither of the detectives. They were somewhere, waiting for him.

He went to the window, unlocked it, then edged it upward. It moved without a sound. Just outside, the steel bands of the fire escape came down from the sixth floor. There was a small landing outside his window and then a stairway down the side to the alley.

Once out of the window and on the fire escape, he moved quickly down to the ground. He paused for a moment, watching both ends of the alley. For a moment he frowned, thinking that he saw movement at the farthest end. He shook his head. He was starting to imagine things. Before he left the room, he had taken out the .38 caliber revolver he carried now for emergencies and pushed the barrel down inside his belt. It felt secure there and would be easy to draw.

He turned and walked toward the near end of the alley where the feeble street lamp glowed. He would soon be away and out on another adventure. Kirby loved the chase, but not when it came as close as it had today. He would never let that happen again.

Twenty yards from the street he stopped and leaned against the building and rested a moment. The clothes bag was heavier than he remembered. He studied the shadows at the end of the alley but could see no lurking detective. They both must be in the hall waiting for him to return to room 303. What a good move that had been getting a second room!

He picked up the bags and hurried ahead. He would not take a cab, since drivers sometimes had good memories. He would walk to the waterfront. It wasn't much over a mile. He could do that, find the right ship that would sail with the dawn and be on board and fast asleep before midnight. Yes!

He came to the mouth of the alley and paused.

"Hold it right there. We're the police. Don't move!"

The words came out of the blackness like a lightning bolt, catching him by total surprise. A woman's voice! So they hadn't stayed in the hallway. They had tricked him.

Kirby dropped his heavy clothing bag, drew his revolver and fired at where he figured the voice was. A shot came in return, digging into his left arm. He cried out in pain but held on the valise and began running. Another shot came after him but missed. He saw a shadow chasing him. He stopped and fired at the shadow. He saw the woman grunt in pain and fall. He turned and raced into the darkness along the unlit street, his feet pounding the sidewalk as fast as they could.

Behind him he again heard someone running. This would be the man; the woman was down. Good. Now it was one to one at least.

He darted up an alley and ran as softly as he could, but his new leather shoes still slapped the ground. He'd have to walk if he wanted to move quietly.

Flavian Kirby knew he couldn't afford to walk. Not now. Not with that lawman following him. He hurried again toward a faint light at the end of the alley. The waterfront had to be in this direction. He ran on.

Chapter Twelve

Flavian Kirby clutched the valise to his chest with both hands as he ran. He was fast losing his breath. The years were catching up with him. He could hear someone behind him. No matter how many alleys he went down or streets he followed, the gent behind seemed to be back there and getting closer. Kirby thought of hiding the valise and giving up. He had no more of the bogus bills in his wallet. There would be no proof against him. But he discarded the idea as stupid. Delphine would identify him as the man who gave her the bogus bills. The lawmen would scour every alley he had used until they found the plates. No, he had to keep running.

At last he could smell the river ahead. Was it still practical or possible to get on a steamer? That could take some time—buying a ticket and finding a cabin. Where would the lawman be?

He had to stop. His lungs burned like the inside of a red-hot stove. His breath came in short gasps and gulps. He backed into a narrow space between two buildings in a dank and dark alley and tried to hold his breath as he heard the running steps come closer.

Then they were past, and he forced himself out of the small space and walked back the way he had just come. He was almost at the end of the long alley when he heard the footsteps coming toward him once more. The lawman had not been fooled.

Just ahead was a pier with a stern wheeler tied up. Flavian raced across the street, walked calmly up the gangplank and vanished in the structure of the big Mississippi river boat.

Spur McCoy had just cleared the edge of the building facing the street when he saw a shadow rush up the gangplank of a boat tied at the dock just across the way. It had to be his man. Where else could he go?

The big boat was preparing to get underway. McCoy raced across the street and jumped over two feet of muddy water, landing on the gangplank as the steamer slowly edged away from the dock.

"You just made it, mate," the gangway man shouted. "You need a ticket. See the purser on deck B."

McCoy hurried to Deck B, up one level, and found the purser's office. He showed his badge.

"I'm chasing a man who just got on board. Did anyone buy a ticket not more than two or three minutes ago?"

The man shook his head. "No sir. Ain't sold a ticket now in an hour."

"You didn't see a small man, about five-four, well-dressed, carrying one valise?"

"Afraid not. You don't need a ticket, you being a government man and all. Good luck in finding him. Just don't disturb any of our cabin passengers."

"Then he didn't rent a cabin?"

"Couldn't. We're full up on both A and B decks."

McCoy thanked him and felt the steamer's big wheel turn faster as they started to plow upstream on the mighty Mississippi. He toured B deck, watching for the dapper little man and the valise. The ship had plenty of lights but there were dark recesses where he could see nothing. He worked the whole deck, saw dozens of strolling passengers, a pair of lovers locked in a kiss, and a man and woman screaming at each other in a good fight.

But no Kirby.

McCoy walked down to A deck, which was nearer water level, and prowled over most of it. Nothing. He went into the big gambling hall midships and worked the crowd there. At least 50 people crowded around gambling tables of all kinds from dice to poker to roulette.

For one fleeting glance he saw a man he thought could be Kirby, but when the man turned around it wasn't. Again he prowled the decks, staring at each cabin as he passed, wondering where the counterfeiter might be. They were out in the channel now, at least a quarter of a mile to shore.

The only thing certain was that Kirby was still on the ship. He hadn't jumped in the Mississippi and swam to shore, not with all of that valuable fake money.

A movement in the shadows ahead caught McCoy's attention. He paused, turned away, then spun around and looked closer. Beside one of the big funnels he saw a person crouched in the shadows.

McCoy drew his six-gun, darted to the spot and grabbed an arm. He pulled out a ten year-old boy who was shivering with fear.

"Don't shoot. Don't shoot me. I know I ain't got no ticket, but I just had to get away from my pa. He beat me something fierce. Figured he'd kill me before I grew up so I sneaked on board and . . ."

McCoy dropped his arm, gave the boy two dollars and returned to the search. Far down along A deck he heard a scream and ran that way. A moment later a cabin door in front of him flew open, and a large man tumbled out and skidded to a stop on his belly. The man tried to get up, but looked back in the cabin and didn't move.

"Close the door," he heard a voice inside order. "Close the door, and I won't kill that no-good husband of yours."

A woman's hand reached out for the door. It had swung outward and automatically latched against the bulkhead. When she leaned around to grab the door, she saw McCoy flat against the bulkhead on the other side of the door.

Instead of grabbing the door, the woman dove out of the room, hit the deck and rolled away out of sight of the person in the cabin.

McCoy edged his six-gun around the door without showing himself. "It's all over, Kirby. Give it up. There's no way out of that cabin, and I'm not moving until you throw out your gun."

For several moments there was a strained silence, then a revolver fired from inside the cabin, and the bullet grazed McCoy's wrist just under the butt of his Peacemaker. Instinctively he fired in return.

Before he could fire again, a flash of white roared past McCoy, ran the eight feet to the rail and dove overboard into the Mississippi.

"Man overboard!" McCoy bellowed. The big paddle behind the boat ran slower and slower. McCoy darted into the room and saw the valise sitting on the bunk. He opened it to be sure it was what he wanted, saw the fake bills and a carefully wrapped bundle and carried the bag out to the deck.

The captain ran up and asked who had called man overboard. McCoy showed him his credentials and said the man was a wanted criminal. The captain ordered two sailors to put a small boat over the side. McCoy, carrying the valise, demanded that he go on the search.

"The man is a federal prisoner and in my control," he told them. They didn't argue. The big boat's blades turned just enough to hold it against the downstream current. A moment later the rowboat was caught by the power of the Mississippi and swept downstream. The big river boat blasted its steam whistle, the huge blades churned the water, and the boat moved on upstream. As the small rowboat drifted downstream, one of the sailors on the oars looked at McCoy.

"You're the captain here, but I'd guess he'd try for the near shore, less than two hundred yards here, but the current would wash him half a mile downstream before he could make it."

"Look where you think we might find him," Spur ordered.

The two sailors pulled for the shore as they drifted down with the current. The night was black as thick smoke. In the distance now he could still see the brightly lighted river boat plowing against the current.

It was some time before McCoy could see the near shoreline, lined with trees and brush.

"Man must have been a good swimmer or he wouldn't have jumped in," the sailor said.

"Don't know," McCoy answered, "but he was over sixty years old. Don't see how he could swim far."

They pulled hard on the oars then and soon came close to the shallows.

"He could walk on in from here," the other sailor said.

"Put me on shore quietly, and I'll look for him along there. You keep working the riverbank. If you find either him or his body, shoot off that flare gun you have in the bow."

McCoy only got wet to his ankles when he stepped into the edge of the Mississippi and walked on to dry land. He jogged along a path by the river for five minutes but found no sign of the counterfeiter.

Put yourself in the other guy's shoes, McCoy told himself. He had the valise, sure now that he had the bulk of the bogus bills and the plates, but not the wanted man. Either he or his drowned body would close the case.

What would he do if he was Kirby and had just managed to swim to shore? He'd have no matches that would work. He'd look for the first light and ask for help. McCoy wondered if the water was so cold the man would die before he could get ashore.

McCoy remembered how the little man had ran. He was fast on his feet. McCoy thought he would be able to chase him down after a block or two, but he hadn't. The little man must be tougher than he looked.

McCoy carried the valise and jogged downstream another 100 yards. This time when he came from behind some trees, he saw lights ahead. There was a cluster of three or four buildings. He approached the first one quietly but saw no muddy or wet footprints on the wooden porch.

He went on and checked all four houses but saw no obvious place where Kirby could have entered.

Next he went to all four houses and peeked in the lighted windows. In the first three he saw nothing out of the ordinary. In one a family of four played dominoes on the kitchen table. In another two older folks sat and rocked and read.

In the third house he found only a mother and a small child breast feeding.

At the last one he saw something strange. The man of the house lay on his stomach on the floor with his hands tied behind his back.

A woman put more wood into an already hot fire in the open fireplace. She seemed ill-at-ease, nervous. McCoy listened but could hear nothing unusual. Then someone coughed, a deep racking sound that sounded like Mississippi river water in a lung.

The woman came back into view with a wet pair of pants and a shirt. She hung them over the backs of wooden chairs and pushed them toward the fireplace.

Had to be Kirby. Did Kirby still have his .38? With the new solid cartridges they would fire just as well wet as dry. Surprise was his best weapon.

McCoy went to the far window, but it did not look in on the living room. The kitchen was dark. He went back to the door, set the valise under the edge of the porch where it couldn't be seen and eased up on the boards.

He moved slowly to the door, making no sound. Thank God this family didn't have a dog. He touched the door knob, praying that it wouldn't be locked. Most of these houses probably didn't even have locks on the doors.

He turned the knob gently with his left hand, unlatching the door. Now he squared with the door and with his right hand lifted his six-gun out of leather and cocked the hammer. Then he rammed the door inward and jumped into the room.

"Don't anyone move!" he bellowed. Everyone froze. He took in the little tableau in a fraction of a second. The woman had just wrung out some underwear in a pan on the living room table. Her husband lay tied at the far end of the room.

Flavian Kirby sat in a chair at the end of the kitchen table wearing the woman's flannel robe. A girl about three sat on his lap, and Kirby's .38 revolver had it's muzzle against the side of her head.

"Welcome to our little group, lawman," Kirby said with a wry smile. "Now don't do anything stupid or this little one never lives to see four years of age. You wouldn't want that on your conscience, would you?"

Spur McCoy growled but slowly lowered his six-gun.

"That's right. Now you just lay that fancy .45 shooter on the floor right beside your foot. First, take it off cock, so it won't go off by accident."

McCoy scowled as he did it. There was nothing else to do right now.

Kirby had combed his wet hair and evidently cleaned the Mississippi mud off of himself. He nodded to the woman. "Alice, you just go right ahead there and get my underdrawers dry so I can be nice and comfortable when I ride out of here. Go on, woman."

She finished wringing out the longjohns and draped them over a chair near the fire.

"Now, suppose you tell me your name, lawman."

"Spur McCoy."

"Good, always fine to know names. This here is Alice. Ain't she a fine one? Look at that saucy little bottom and them good tits. We gonna have play time after a while. Over there all tied up on the floor is George who's a mite testy right now. This little one is Cindy. So, now we know each other.

"Alice, you get some more of that twine and tie Mr. McCoy's hands behind his back. Do that for me, darling."

She frowned but took twine from the table. McCoy moved his hands behind him. He was outsmarted for the moment, but that didn't mean any of these innocent folks had to die.

When McCoy was tied, the shorter man came up to him and snorted.

"You don't look so fucking good now, lawman. What bunch you with in Washington?"

"Secret Service."

"Ha, protector of the currency. Suppose you know I slaved in that Bureau of Engraving and Printing for damn near thirty years. Left me damn near broke."

He held the .38 by the handle and slashed the barrel into McCoy's belly, making him gasp for breath.

"Yeah, McCoy, not a bigshot Secret Service agent now, are you? Lay down over there besides good old George."

McCoy did. At least his feet weren't tied. He turned so he could look at George and nodded. "Give me some time," he whispered.

Kirby stared at the group. He pulled the chairs back a little from the fire so his clothes wouldn't burn, then he carried the small girl and pushed Alice ahead of him into another room. "Time for bed for little Cindy here. We'll lock her door from the outside so she don't bother us none."

He and Alice were back a moment later. "Now, Alice, you're being a good girl. Suppose you go right on being good and I won't have to shoot old George over there, right?"

Alice was in her late twenties, a little thick at the waist with large breasts and a small saucy bottom as Kirby had described her.

"You'll do whatever I tell you to do so old George over there doesn't get shot, right?"

"Yes," she said softly.

"Good, strip yourself down to your waist. I want to see them good-looking tits you got."

Her face registered surprise and shock. "You never said I'd have to do nothing like that."

Kirby cocked the .38 revolver and aimed it at George. Quickly the woman unbuttoned her blouse and tore it off, then took off a chemise and unwound a wrapper that held her big breasts in place. They fell out like two sacks of spilled watermelons.

"My God, what big tits!" Kirby said. "Bring them over here, Alice. Nothing a husband hates more than to see another man at his wife. Sit down here on the table and let me play with them suckers. Them is really a fine pair."

McCoy had turned slightly and pushed his hands toward George.

"Try and untie them," McCoy whispered.

George moved his hands a little and touched the twine. This had to work. McCoy figured if it didn't, all of them except little Cindy had about a half hour to live.

Chapter Thirteen

"Alice didn't tie you tight," George whispered. "Making progress."

"Shut up, you two," Flavian Kirby said. "You're interrupting my gnawing on these big tits. Damn they are fine ones."

"Don't think about it," McCoy whispered. "If you don't get me free, we're both dead men and Alice along with us."

Kirby had settled in to devouring the woman. He sucked and chewed and licked on her breasts as he pulled down her dress and the rest of her clothing. Soon she was naked, and he grinned.

"Hell, not bad for a quick one. Hey, George, you got some hot pussy of a woman here. She's cunt damp already."

George stopped working on Spur's hands when he saw Flavian look over his shoulder.

"Don't hurt her," George pleaded.

"Hell, a couple of pokings never hurt any little gal. Get yourself down on the floor, woman. I like it rough once in a while."

George tugged on the twine, and McCoy pulled and twisted his hands and wrists to help matters. He looked over and saw the woman flat on her back and Kirby trying to get her legs spread. McCoy felt one of the loops give.

"Yes, that's it, faster," McCoy whispered.

Kirby yelped in delight as he spread Alice's legs apart and knelt between them. He fumbled at his crotch as he whipped the robe away and went down on her.

"Oh, yes, you are ready, Alice. You hot little cunt. You'd take on any man who got you naked. Admit it now, wouldn't you?"

She didn't answer but just turned her head away. McCoy could see that her eyes were closed.

Another strand of twine loosened. McCoy tugged and pulled at his hands until his arms ached. Slowly his right hand slid past the twine and more of the loops loosened.

Kirby drove forward and gave a big yelp of pleasure.

"Damn, but you're tight. Don't he ever get into you? Hell, I'd have you twice a day if'n I was his age."

McCoy could see Kirby's rear end under the robe pumping back and forth. At his age it should take him a few minutes to get his pleasure fulfilled.

McCoy gave one more pull and his right hand came free. Quickly he undid the rest of the twine, then reached over and untied George's hands.

"Now," McCoy whispered. Both men lunged up from the floor and charged Kirby. When he saw them coming he pulled out and rolled away from them. His right hand grabbed his six-gun and he got off one shot before Alice clubbed his wrist with both of her fisted hands and the gun flew to the floor.

It was too far away for him to reach. Alice kicked it away with her bare foot, and it skittered toward the two charging men.

Faster than McCoy figured possible, Kirby bolted for the door, opened it and charged into the night.

George went to his wife, kissed her and held her in his arms. McCoy grabbed his own six-gun, then the one from the floor and rushed out the door after the counterfeiter. He couldn't get far. He was barefooted and in a woman's pink robe.

McCoy stopped and listened and heard soft sounds as if running bare feet were heading toward the next house. McCoy fired a shot into the air in that direction, then raced after the fugitive.

He saw no door open on the next house, so he ran past it. Then he stopped and listened again. Ahead at the next house he saw a sliver of light break up the night, then vanish. A door had opened. Was it a coincidence, or had Kirby rushed inside?

McCoy sprinted to the house and looked in the window. It was a couple and two children still playing dominoes at the kitchen table.

Standing in front of them was Flavian Kirby pretending he had a gun under his robe. As McCoy watched the man inside stood, bellowed in anger and swung at the smaller man. Kirby ducked and raced out of the room to the rear of the house. McCoy tore around the side of the house but could see nothing in the moonless night.

He listened.

Soft footsteps moved away into a grove of trees and brush toward the river. McCoy fired once in that direction and charged ahead. He reached the spot where he figured Kirby should be, but no one was there. The thick brush along the Mississippi was hard enough to work through in daylight; now at night it would be nearly impossible to make good time or try to find someone inside it.

McCoy tried the outside approach. He listened to the sounds of Kirby working through the brush. A stick snapped now and then, and the branch of a tree creaked and groaned as it was pushed aside.

McCoy moved along the open stretch just outside the brush, listening and waiting.

The sounds of movement in the brush continued for half an hour, then stopped, and McCoy decided that Kirby had stopped to get a little rest, maybe some sleep. He had no idea what time it was, but he wasn't about to light a match to check his watch. He tried to see the stars but there was enough scattering of clouds to block out the North Star so he couldn't judge the time by the position of the Big Dipper that moved around the North Star every night.

He sat on the ground and waited.

Twice he nodded off but came awake the moment he started to roll to the ground.

It was a long night. He saw the stars fade and then a false dawn with streaks of light from the east. At last the darkness was eaten up by the rising sun, and McCoy moved behind a large maple tree on the fringes of the brush. Now he could see a quarter mile stretch of the brushline and not be spotted himself.

McCoy figured if he was Kirby, he'd have had enough of the brush with no shoes on and would strike out for the trail along the river, watching for an unsuspecting household where he could get some clothes, a gun and maybe a hostage or two.

McCoy waited another half hour, then he took a stroll along the trail, listening for any sounds. There were no indications that Kirby was moving through the brush. Maybe there was a dirt flat where he could run without any noise.

McCoy walked downstream faster. He saw a rider coming along the road a quarter of a mile ahead. Realizing the danger the horse presented, McCoy sprinted forward, but his move came too late.

A figure in a pink robe darted out from some brush and caught the bridle of the horse. A moment later the young woman had been pulled down, and Kirby mounted the animal, turned it and raced away.

McCoy ran up to the girl on the ground.

"Miss, I'm a law officer. Is there another horse nearby? That man is a wanted felon. I'm trying to capture him."

She was not yet 20, plain with long dark hair. She wiped her eyes, jumped up and nodded.

"Back there at my Pa's place. He's got two horses all saddled. They were gonna follow me."

100 yards around a bend and past some brush was a small house, barn and corral. Two saddled mounts stood at a rail in front of the house.

McCoy jumped into the saddle and called to the girl. "I'll bring your horses back, promise." Then he raced after the fleeing Kirby. He couldn't do much without clothes or shoes, except run and hide. If he came to a town he'd be at a disadvantage.

But there was no town. McCoy galloped his mount for a quarter of a mile, then eased her down, picked up the hoofprints of the horse ahead of him and walked the mare for a quarter of a mile. He couldn't see any horseman ahead.

He could track at a lope. The ground along the river was soft, even wet in spots, and Kirby was pushing the horse too fast. It couldn't last long.

After another half mile the trail wound around a curve in the river, and on a slight downhill stretch McCoy saw the fugitive. His horse had broken down, and Kirby was standing beside it. When he looked back and saw a rider coming, he ran into the brush along the Mississippi.

McCoy rode to the spot and saw that there was a small stream that emptied into the mighty river here. He rode along it and stared in surprise. Just across the stream was a small fishing shack. A black man lay on the porch trying to stand up.

Kirby sat in a rowboat 50 feet into the Mississippi, rowing farther into the current that swept him downstream.

There was no other boat there.

He'd have to follow him on land. In a heartbeat McCoy knew that was all he could do. If he had a rifle he could shoot the little boat into kindling. If he came to a house, he'd try to borrow a rifle.

McCoy found it easy to follow the progress of the rowboat. At this point the water slowed and the river widened. Sometimes the current carried Kirby toward the far shore, sometimes to the near one. McCoy tried to stay out of sight as much as possible.

He didn't want the counterfeiter to get the idea of going to the other side of the wide river and escaping that way.

Another mile down the river speeded up. The current swung toward McCoy's shore, and he saw Kirby fighting to stay away from the shoreline. He lost the fight.

McCoy saw his chance. The current would swing the little boat within 50 feet of the shoreline. He loaded a sixth round in his Peacemaker, rode for the point of land ahead where the small craft would sweep by and waded ten feet into the shallow shore ledge.

The rowboat swept toward him, and he spotted the hump of the pink robe. When the boat came closest to the shore, McCoy fired. He aimed not at the man but at the waterline of the small boat. The big .45 shells whacked into the dry wood of the boat and tore open holes. Five of the six rounds ripped into the side of the boat, and he heard a yelp of surprise from Kirby.

McCoy fired the rest of the rounds from the .38 but he wasn't sure any of them hit the boat. He saw Kirby sit up in the boat and shake his fist at McCoy, then he began scooping water out of the craft with his hands.

"Good, it's leaking," McCoy said out loud. He ran back to his horse and followed the shoreline as close as possible. Now he could see the boat settling lower in the Mississippi. He had to go around a patch of brush, and when he came back he didn't see anyone in the boat.

Where did he go?

Then a head popped up for a look. Kirby had to be lying in the water. McCoy had reloaded his six-gun and fired six more times at the boat, but it was beyond his range.

The boat sank lower in the water. Five minutes later McCoy paced the boat as it last sank under the muddy flow. Kirby flopped out of it like a dead fish, then began to swim for shore. He was an expert swimmer, and even with the current moving him downstream he made good progress. Less than a quarter of a mile down the river, Kirby staggered up from the mud flats along the shore and fell on the hard ground.

He looked up at McCoy and snorted. "Big win for you, McCoy. So you captured me. What's so earth-shattering here? Was I going to rip apart the economy with my $88,000."

"You were hurting a lot of good people. Did you ever think of that?"

Spur made Kirby walk. He had lost the robe in the water and walked naked as a bluejay along the country road. In the distance, McCoy saw a small town. The agent took off his shirt and let Kirby wrap it around his waist to cover his privates.

A half hour later, McCoy had Kirby deposited in the small town's one jail cell in the police station. The town marshal swore on a stack of beer bottles that he would guard the man with his life. There was only one key to the cell.

McCoy asked to see it, then put it in his pocket.

"Hey, what if the jail catches fire? How do we get this man out?"

"Put out the fire," McCoy said and went to a café for a solid meal.

An hour and a half later he was back where he had borrowed the horse. He told them what had happened to the first horse. "Looked like she foundered, but I didn't see her on the road, so she may have recovered and be down along the river about a mile." He thanked them and moved north.

He walked on back to the home of George and Alice and little Cindy where he had first found Kirby.

They all sat at the kitchen table eating a noon meal. George went to the door and invited him in. Right away Alice blushed and rushed into another room.

"She's still touchy about your seeing her naked and all," George said.

McCoy said that he understood and that he had just come back to get something he left under the steps. He went back outside and looked, but the valise wasn't there.

George held up his hands before McCoy could accuse him.

"We figured all that money was that Kirby guy's and that he owed us plenty for what he did to us—raping Alice and all."

"Where is it?" McCoy asked, his voice low and level and deadly.

"Oh, we got it. We don't want all of it, but we figure fair is fair. We'll split with that Mr. Kirby. We'll keep half, and he can have half of it back."

McCoy told him the bills were all counterfeit and not worth the paper it cost to print them.

"No, can't be!" George thundered. "I seen lots of paper money. This is genuine as rain."

"Notice the serial numbers on the bills?"

George shook his head.

"They are all the same. They were all printed from the same plate stolen from the mint in Washington D.C. Bring out the valise and I'll show you."

George brought the valise out of another room.

"Still say it's good as gold."

McCoy broke one of the bands around the bills and laid six of them out so the serial numbers showed one after another. The numbers were identical.

"You ever see two pieces of paper money with the same number on them before," McCoy asked.

"Oh, shit!"

"Afraid so. Now if you have any of these bills, you best bring them and put them back in the valise. Otherwise you'll be breaking the law by passing counterfeit money. That would put you in federal prison for ten long years."

"Oh, damn!"

Alice came through the door with a handful of the bills. "We was just aiming to go into the city and spend us some money." She scowled. "Reckon now that we can't.

"But look how we helped you," George said. "I untied your hands, and Alice there slammed Kirby's hand when he was shooting and got the gun away from him. That's got to be worth something."

McCoy took a deep breath. He'd figure out some way to cover it. He dug into his pocket, took out his wallet and lifted three good $20 bills out. He handed them to Alice.

"Here, Alice. You go to town and buy yourself something pretty. Get a new shirt for George, maybe."

She grinned. "I thank you, sir."

McCoy looked back in the valise. He better check to be sure the missing engraving plates were there as well. He found the small wrapped package and opened it. It wasn't the plates but rather a packet of what must be family pictures. He identified one of the people as Kirby.

So where the hell were the engraving plates that Flavian Kirby had stolen?

Chapter Fourteen

By the time McCoy rented a horse and rode back to the small town of Cloverville where he had left the counterfeiter, the town marshal had rustled up a pair of pants, a shirt and some shoes for the prisoner.

They weren't near as fancy as those Flavian Kirby usually wore. He sat in the corner of the cell with his eyes closed.

"Now's the time to tell me, Kirby. What did you do with the plates?"

"I eat off plates."

"You know what I mean—the engraving plates front and back of the twenty dollar bill you stole from the mint."

"You'll never find them."

"Neither will you, Kirby. You'll be in jail for forty years, if you live that long."

"Don't matter. I had my time. I had my fun. I proved that a man who was smart enough could outwit the whole United States government."

"For a while, that is, Kirby. So why not give us the plates?"

"Never can tell where they might be. Maybe I sent them to Paris where some of the best counterfeiters in the world can turn out a billion dollars in twenties and flood the world market and collapse the U.S. economy."

"The bills won't pass that well in large numbers, Kirby. You know that. Not with the same serial number."

"Sure I know, but that don't put you no closer to getting the plates."

"You can talk here or back in St. Louis or in Washington. It's up to you."

By the time McCoy decided that Kirby wasn't going to talk in the jail cell, it was after suppertime. The town marshal allowed as how there wasn't a hotel in their small town, McCoy was more than welcome to have supper at his house and sleep in the spare room.

The next morning, McCoy handcuffed Kirby to the side of a rented carriage and drove back to St. Louis. He deposited Kirby in the city jail and then wired Washington D.C. with the fact that Kirby was in custody and most of the $88,000 in bogus bills had been recovered. The problem was that the engraving plates were missing.

A return wire came almost before McCoy got out of the telegraph office.

"TO MCCOY. CAPITAL INVESTIGATIONS, ST.

LOUIS. MO. MUST RECOVER THE MISSING $20 ENGRAVINGS. DON'T WANT THIS TO HAPPEN AGAIN. REPEAT. MUST RECOVER THE PLATES. SENDING. W.D. HALLECK. WASHINGTON."

Back at the office he found Jessica. Her wound on her upper arm was slight and was bandaged. She wanted all the details about Kirby's capture which he told her. Then McCoy and Jessica went back to Kirby's room in the hotel. It was the only bet they had. Maybe they could find a lead in the counterfeiter's room which had been sealed by the St. Louis police.

It took them three hours to go over the room inch by inch. They looked on the bottom of the dresser drawers, under a picture on the wall and even inside the water pitcher.

They sat on the unmade bed and pondered.

"What if he didn't have the plates with him?" McCoy suggested. "Say this was just a swing around the country to build up his supply of good money by passing bills."

"So where did he live in Chicago and Washington?" Jessica asked.

"When we're through here, I'll have someone check."

"Are we through here?" Jessica asked. She looked at the bed and grinned. "We don't have to be through. I mean, we could close the door and lock it and make some use of this bed."

He kissed her lips gently. "Later. Something has to be here to lead us to those damn plates."

"Maybe he hid them somewhere and memorized the spot," she said.

"Possible. Maybe he stored them with some of his books and furniture."

"Possible," Jessica said.

McCoy stood and slammed his hand against the side of the dresser. "Hell, the plates could be anywhere."

"What was that?" Jessica asked.

"What was what?"

"Something just fell down from behind the dresser."

McCoy went to his knees and saw a crumpled piece of paper.

"It must have been wedged behind the dresser. When you moved it, the paper fell."

They spread out the paper slowly. The handwriting was neat and perfectly formed, the way an engraver would write. It took McCoy a moment to figure out what it said.

"Mr. Lance Whitmore, 124 Chesterton Lain." Then there were some random marks.

"What in the world?" Jessica asked.

"The name will be easy enough to trace, especially with the address. Are you familiar with Chesterton Lane near Washington? It's a fine residential street. A lot of government people live there. Evidently Kirby started to write a letter to this Whitmore. Remember Kirby is an engraver, an expert at perfection. When he misspelled the word "lane", he was angry, wadded up the paper and threw it away."

He grabbed her hand, and they hurried out of the room. McCoy led them straight to the telegraph office and sent a wire to the general.

"TO GEN. HALLECK. CAPITAL INVESTIGA-TIONS, WASHINGTON, D.C. CHECK BACK-

GROUND AND OCCUPATION OF LANCE
WHITMORE, 124 CHESTERTON LANE, D.C.
A DISCREET INQUIRY. MAY BE SOME CON-
NECTION WITH FLAVIAN KIRBY CASE. REPLY
SOONEST. SENDING. MCCOY."

"I still don't understand," Priscilla said when they
got back to the office and showed her the paper.
"Why should a part of an address and a name be so
important?"

Jessica explained. "If you were in a strange town and
had something extremely valuable that you didn't want
to carry with you any more, what might you do with it?
You have no home address to mail it to, but you could
wrap it up and mail it to a good friend or someone who
would keep it for you until you asked for it without any
questions."

"Another member of the gang?"

"Could be," McCoy said. "Until we learn something from Washington about who this man is, we
won't know."

"How long will that take?" Jessica asked.

"An hour, a day—who knows?" McCoy said. "But
I've a hunch the general is worried enough about those
plates that he'll get a check made as fast as he can."

By that time it was nearing 5:00 o'clock. They told
Priscilla she could go on home and take care of her
father. Jessica and Spur ate that evening in the hotel
dining room which wasn't known for it's excellent
food but had fast service.

Just after 7:00 o'clock they went back to her room,
and Jessica locked the door. McCoy slid a chair back
under the knob and wedged it in solidly.

"Why, Mr. McCoy, it appears that you have some sort of wild and crazy plans for the rest of the evening."

"Just trying to protect you from the lawless outsiders," he said with a grin.

She grabbed him and kissed him, and they fell on the bed laughing. He undressed her gently and slowly, kissing away every article of clothing until she was squirming naked and excited on the big bed.

Then she sat up and undressed him, teasing him along the way until by the time she had his pants off, his erection was full and throbbing.

"Right now!" she cried and went to her hands and knees and looked back over her shoulder. McCoy grinned, knelt behind her tight little bottom and spread her cheeks to find the right slot. He nudged into her gently, slowly, listening to her moaning in front of him.

When he was fully entered, he caught the right angle of her hip and her belly and held on as he thrust back and fourth.

"More, more," she wailed. "Faster, you slowpoke, or I'll beat you to home plate again." Then she writhed under him, her body shattered by a thousand vibrations as spasm after spasm racked her frame until she nearly collapsed. He held her up and continued to drive into her. His own satisfaction came quickly but not before she was spurred into another wild series of climaxes that overshadowed his own brief leap into ecstacy.

Then slowly she eased forward until she lay on her stomach with him still in her.

"Don't move or I'll kill you," she said from where her head nearly vanished in the soft pillow.

Neither of them said a word for three or four minutes, then he withdrew from her and lay beside her on the bed.   •

"So how did you like your first case working with a woman agent?" she asked.

"Better than I expected. Although I did have to rescue you once."

"True, but I saw the vital piece of evidence fall from behind the dresser."

"Right, but I would have . . ."

She put her fingers over his lips to quiet him.

"Let's not get into any arguments. This case is probably about over for me. I have a feeling that the plates won't be that hard to find."

"Why, Jessica?"

"If you owned those plates, who would you send them to for safekeeping?"

"A good friend or an accomplice."

"Right. You said good friend first. My guess is that this Mr. Whitmore is exactly that—a good friend. I'd address the letter to him, enclose the plates all wrapped up and put in the letter that this was something special that I wanted Whitmore to save for me until I could get back to D.C. to pick it up."

"You might be right. If so, that means that the government people in Washington should have the plates by tonight," McCoy said."

"If this Whitmore cooperates. It could take a search warrant from a federal judge to get into his house. By that time, Whitmore might check out what was in that secret envelope and decide to do something with it on his own."

"Guess why we came to your room tonight?"

She grinned, sat up and pushed one breast into his mouth. "Could it be because a telegram marked urgent would be delivered directly to your room even if it comes late at night, and it could disturb something important going on inside your room?"

"Close enough," he said after he came away from her breast which showed delicate teeth marks.

A sudden knocking on the door brought them both upright. He motioned for her to answer it. She walked naked to the door.

"Yes, what is it?"

A voice shouted something, but neither of them could understand the words. Carefully, Jessica took the chair away, unlocked the door and edged it open an inch.

"Yes, what do you want?"

The door burst open as a shoulder hit it, bouncing Jessica back a step. Priscilla marched into the room, nodded at both of them, closed the door, locked it and replaced the chair.

She reached for the buttons at the front of her blouse and began undoing them.

"I've had about enough of being ignored. I mean, here I am a bright young person with a rather good body and full breasts and I am ignored by the sexiest man I know. I won't stand for it any longer. I'm here to say that if you don't want me, then tell me that after I get my clothes off."

McCoy sat on the bed, staring at her. He couldn't find anything to say.

Jessica watched with her mouth open as Priscilla stripped off her blouse and her chemise and thrust out her bare breasts at them.

"I can go naked, too," Priscilla said.

McCoy chuckled, and it broke the tension in the room. "Priscilla, little darling, long as you made such a bold first move, the game is wide open. Welcome aboard."

Jessica laughed, too. "Honey, I'm glad you came. We can have a great party the rest of the night. We'll worry about the damn counterfeiting plates tomorrow."

By then, Priscilla had shucked out of the rest of her clothes, and for a minute as she stood there naked, she became shy. She turned away from them, hiding herself, then took a deep breath and spun around.

"I don't want you to think I'm a virgin or anything like that. I've had sex with a man before."

McCoy grinned. "Exactly how many times, Pris?"

"How many?" She went over to the bed and sat down beside McCoy. Jessica sat close to him on the other side. Both women reached for his growing erection.

"How many men have you fucked, Pris?" Jessica asked.

"Well, you want to know exactly?"

"If you can remember," McCoy said.

She watched them, and then her chin tilted up a little as McCoy had seen so many times. "Once, one time when I was fifteen and neither of us knew what we were trying to do."

Spur chuckled, reached over and kissed her cheek. Jessica kissed her cheek, too. Pris shook her red hair, turned to McCoy and kissed him on the lips, then she pushed him down on the bed and lay on top of him.

"Oh, gracious! You'll never guess how many times I've dreamed of doing this."

Jessica sat on one side of the bed and watched. "Looks like it's your turn right now, little Pris. Enjoy."

Priscilla rolled off McCoy and lay huddled on the bed. When he reached over and kissed her lips, she responded shyly. Then he bent and kissed one breast, and she trembled. He kissed the other orb, then licked around her nipple and bit it tenderly.

Priscilla trembled, then her whole body vibrated with a storm of spasms drilling through her small frame.

"Oh, glory! Oh, God! Oh, McCoy!" She pulled him on top of her, and he cushioned her until it was over. Her eyes were wide as she stared up at him.

"Never felt anything like that before," Priscilla said. She pulled him down. "Now, put it inside me. I want to see what that feels like. I hardly remember from before."

Gently he entered her. She yelped in sudden pain, then her smile broke through and her arms encircled him and she cried for joy.

"So wonderful! Why didn't you tell me it would be this good? Why haven't I been doing this before? Oh, damn, I'm going to do it again!"

She climaxed again with the same array of moans and vibrations, and her little bottom danced on the bed, pounding upward a dozen times toward the end.

"Wonderful! That's just the most marvelous feeling that I can ever remember having. It's absolutely pure heaven!"

McCoy knew that Jessica had moved. Now he could feel her finger searching for his tight little bung. She found it at about the same time he started his climax and he finished with her watching every stroke he made.

Below them, Priscilla lay there with her arms at her sides. She smiled at them in a way neither had ever seen before. "Shame on you, Spur McCoy, for not sharing this joy, this wonder, this marvelous fucking with me before. I know that we're just getting started and that I'm new to this, but I think this is the most wonderful and marvelous and tremendous night of my life!"

They came apart, and the three of them lay on the bed.

"This is pleasant," Jessica said. "The three of us sharing together this way. Everyone has to promise that by morning we'll still be the best of friends. Whether this ever happens again is something we don't need to think about right now."

"I'll say amen to that," McCoy chimed in.

"Oh, me too, me too," Priscilla said, reaching for Spur McCoy's limp privates, trying to get him hard again.

McCoy's mind was distracted for a moment. He knew that they shouldn't be here. The office should be covered. Right at that moment he was sure that a night letter had been slipped under his door two floors below. He wondered what it said, but he was damned if he was going to go get it until morning.

Chapter Fifteen

Spur McCoy unlocked his hotel room door beside the office at 6:30 the next morning and saw the yellow and black envelope where it had been slid under his door sometime during the night. He picked it up and tore it open.

"TO SPUR MCCOY, CAPITAL INVESTIGATIONS, CLAYMORE HOTEL, ST. LOUIS, MISSOURI. RUSH TO WASHINGTON ON NEXT AVAILABLE TRAIN. BRING PRISONER IN CUFFS AND UNDER GUARD. AGENT FLANDERS TO TRAVEL WITH YOU. DEVELOPMENTS HERE RE YOUR LAST WIRE. NEED YOU HERE FOR THE WRAP-UP. REPLY SOONEST. GENERAL WILTON D. HALLECK. WASHINGTON DC SENDING."

McCoy studied the wire, then went back to the third floor where he had spent the night and knocked on the door. A sleepy, frowsy-headed Jessica answered.

"Oh, I was hoping it was you."

He waved the telegram at her. "Night letter from the general. Get dressed to travel and pack. Both of us and Kirby have been ordered to come to Washington on the next train. I'll go wire the general and make arrangements to get Kirby out of the jail. You be ready in an hour."

He turned and walked down the hall, leaving Jessica in momentary confusion.

It took them two hours to make connections for a train heading for Washington, to get their bags on board and to get the St. Louis police to bring Kirby in handcuffs and make sure he was secure in the hands of the federal officers. McCoy signed the prisoner transfer notice and handed it back to the St. Louis roundsman just as the train started to move.

They settled into two compartments, one for the two men and one for Jessica. The train was the Atlantic Flyer, a passengers-only train that had been listed as an express which stopped at selected terminals along the line.

McCoy handcuffed Kirby to the berth, made sure there was no possible means he could use to get away and settled down to read a fresh copy of the *New York Times*. It would be over 800 miles to the nation's capital. Even on this express it would take nearly a day and a half. Jessica came into the compartment shortly, and they played poker for matches, at last allowing Kirby to play, but minus the matches.

"Our job is to deliver you safely to my boss in Washington, Kirby. Nothing you can do will stop me from getting you there. So just relax and accept it. Your fun and games are over."

They left St. Louis shortly before ten o'clock and wired ahead their expected arrival time.

It still took the full day and a half they had been told. They spent the time in a dozen ways, none of them sexual, and at last turned a grousing Flavian Kirby over to Secret Service agents at the Washington central depot shortly after four in the afternoon.

General Halleck and two of his men were there to greet the prisoner and the two agents. It had been three years since Spur McCoy had seen the general who was in his late sixties now, ramrod straight and with a full beard and moustache neatly trimmed and turning gray. His dark brown eyes snapped as he looked at Kirby, then waved him away. General Halleck was a little over five-feet-ten, wore a somber black suit and a stiff collar and tie with his white shirt. His black shoes were polished to a military sheen.

"Good job, McCoy, Flanders. We wanted Kirby here to try to question him. This thing has grown a little out of bounds. Do you have any idea who the man is you had us investigate?"

"No sir," both agents said almost in unison.

"For your information, Lance Whitmore is one of the President's fair-haired boys. He was appointed to the number three post in the Bureau of Engraving and Printing. I have a sheaf of material on the man, but he seems to be on vacation right now somewhere in the Blue Mountains of Virginia."

"Convenient," McCoy murmured.

"Damned lot more than convenient. We've consulted with the president who's given us approval to get a search warrant to the Whitmore house and grounds. I wanted you here to help us work on Kirby and, if needed, go into the mountains."

"I've done my best on Kirby. He isn't going to say a word. He didn't even flinch when we mentioned the Whitmore name."

They walked to a large closed coach and the three of them got in. A driver whipped the rig away without instructions.

"It seems that this Whitmore used to work at one time with Kirby. Both of them are about the same age. Whitmore's work records are being scrutinized. He had no firm control where he could have stolen anything, but still it's a worry."

"Bet the president is a bit grim," Jessica said.

"He's angry, wants it settled quickly one way or the other," the general said.

"How long has Whitmore been on his vacation," McCoy asked.

The general looked at his notes a moment. "About two weeks. He's due back in six days."

McCoy nodded. To him it didn't make sense that Whitmore could be a conspirator. If he'd been gone two weeks, that meant he had left long before Kirby had showed up in St. Louis and probably before Kirby could have mailed the plates to him—if that's what he did mail. They were riding the tails of several assumptions here. He kept this all to himself. Time enough to bring it up later.

They rumbled up to the headquarters of the Secret Service, a small granite building just a block and a half from the White House. The carriage rolled through a guarded gate at the back of the building and stopped.

They got out, and McCoy looked around. The place hadn't changed much.

"Come inside and I'll show you what we've found out about this Whitmore. Not too encouraging, I'm afraid."

In a meeting room with a blackboard, McCoy and Jessica looked at what had been written in chalk on the board. It was a work history of Lance Whitmore.

The general took over the briefing. "He came with the Bureau of Engraving and Printing about fifteen years ago. Worked in the same department as Kirby.

"Later promoted to junior engraver, and two years later promoted again into management at a junior level. Then he quit for five years and worked for a big bank here in Washington and got shoulder deep into the political whirl.

"Two years ago he was appointed to the post of number three man at the bureau with wide-ranging powers, yet still with several checks on him."

A knock sounded on the door. It opened discreetly. The general glanced that way and nodded. "That's all the time we have for your briefing. We're on our way to serve the papers and search the Whitmore place on Chesterton Lane. Interesting how you came on this whole connection. Let's hope it pays off for us."

Jessica and McCoy followed the general out of the room and were soon back in the same plush coach. This time there were four more rigs that followed them out of the yard behind the building. Half of the men carried shotguns. All were armed in some way.

"I assume both of you have your weapons," the general said. They nodded. "Good. Probably won't need them, but never can tell."

Ten minutes later they pulled up in front of 124 Chesterton Lane. The general sat in his coach and glanced out. Four men drifted from the carriages into the shrubbery and to the rear of the house. Two more men went to each side. Then someone tapped the general's door.

"Let's find out what this is all about," General Halleck said.

He held an envelope in his gloved hand as they marched up the sidewalk, through a fancy iron gate and up the steps to a three-story house that was well-painted with carefully trimmed grounds.

The general rang a twist bell that set up a clatter somewhere in the house. A moment later a maid in uniform answered the door.

"I'm sorry but Mr. and Mrs. Whitmore are vacationing in the mountains. I can take a message for them."

"I'm General Halleck of the United States Secret Service. This is a search warrant granted by the federal district court allowing us to search the premises and adjoining area."

The girl took the envelope and nodded. "Well, I've heard of you. I guess you can go ahead and search."

"Girl, where is the mail that has arrived for the Whitmores since they've been away?"

"Oh, it's all in a safe box. I'm to put it in there every

day when it comes and lock it."

"Would you show us, please?" Jessica asked the frightened girl. She looked at Jessica, shivered and led them into a study on the first floor.

The place was furnished in good taste with a few expensive pieces but nothing lavish, McCoy noticed. The study was lined with books and was a little ostentatious. Probably painting a better picture of the man of the house.

The maid pointed to a lock box, a kind of home safe that sat to one side. It had a wide door and a combination lock.

"I'll ask you to open the safe," General Halleck said. "You'll be in no trouble with your employer for doing so. I'll see to that myself."

The girl turned the knobs. McCoy looked away so he wouldn't remember the combination. A moment later he heard the lock click, and the girl opened the wide door. Inside was a box a foot square half-filled with letters, larger envelopes, a flyer or two and one newspaper.

The general pulled the box from the safe and set it on the walnut desk top. He sorted through the material, scanning each item, then putting it to one side on the desk.

About half way into the pile he smiled and showed an envelope to McCoy.

"It has a St. Louis postmark on it from six days ago, it has six cents in postage, and it's heavy."

He gathered McCoy, Jessica and two other agents who had come in with them.

"You're my witnesses that I'm opening this mail addressed to one Lance Whitmore of 124 Chesterton

Lane." He tore off the top end of the envelope and let the contents fall out on the desk. When one item hit with a heavy clunk, they all smiled.

There was a letter and another item wrapped in several pieces of paper. The general opened the sealing tape on the heavy paper around the wrapped item. He unfolded the paper and smiled. He had them, the front and back engraved plates of the U.S. $20 treasury note.

McCoy picked up the letter that lay to one side, read it and passed it quickly to the general.

"St. Louis, October 12. You'll probably be surprised to hear from me, but I'm traveling again. Remember how we used to dream about seeing the West? I'm on my way to San Francisco.

"Enclosed are some items I want you to keep for me. Nowhere in the West does it seem safe to keep things in a person's room on in a poor excuse for a hotel vault. The items are sealed in heavy paper inside the outer envelope, so you won't need to be concerned with what they are. If you could put them in your safe I'd appreciate it.

"Next time that I'm in town, I'll stop by for dinner on me and we'll talk about old times. Hope all is well with your growing political career. Stay healthy. Sincerely, Flavian Kirby."

The general finished reading it and stared at McCoy. "So, Agent McCoy, what's your evaluation of the letter?"

"I'd say it's just what it appears to be. Whitmore was a friend, a trusted friend he could count on doing as asked without peeking in the envelope. I'd say

Mr. Whitmore has no connection whatsoever with the counterfeiting."

"You may be right. On the other hand the letter could be loaded with coded words and secret instructions. I want Whitmore picked up and brought back to my office as quickly as possible."

He turned to the open-mouthed maid who still stood by the door.

"Miss, do you have an address where your employer can be located in case of a problem here at the house?

She nodded, reached in her pocket, took out a folded piece of paper and handed it to the general. He opened it, read it and handed it to McCoy.

"Here's is your next assignment. Go get him and bring him back without a word what this is all about. I want to question him myself before he knows anything about any of this. Whatever you do, don't discuss the counterfeiting or Kirby."

"Why shall I say he needs to return to Washington at once?" McCoy asked.

"Tell him we have a small crisis in his department and his chief asked me to locate him and have him return."

"Shall I take Agent Flanders with me?"

"You feel you need backup on a peaceful messenger service job such as this?"

"No sir."

McCoy turned and strode out of the room, winking at Jessica as he passed her.

It took McCoy a day and a half to find Whitmore. He took a stage to Fort Royal and rented a horse for the last

20 miles. When he reached the rustic cabin, Whitmore was cleaning fish on the bench near a small lake.

"A crisis in my department! Enough said. I'll be dressed to travel in fifteen minutes. My wife and children can stay the rest of the time and then come back. My wife is most resourceful. Can you tell me anything more about this problem?"

McCoy said his only instructions were to tell Mr. Whitmore of the crisis and ask him to return as quickly as possible.

They rented a buggy at a nearby village and soon were on the stage heading for Washington. McCoy watched the man, but he seemed no more upset than anyone would be who had received such news about his department. They spoke little as the coach sped along.

The third day after he left, McCoy reported to the Secret Service office with Lance Whitmore in tow.

General Halleck greeted him at the door of his big office and asked Whitmore to sit down.

"I don't understand, General Halleck. I was told there is a crisis in my department at the Bureau."

"Indeed there is, Mr. Whitmore. That's exactly what we need to talk about. First a little background. I understand that you know a man named Flavian Kirby."

"Kirby, Kirby. Yes. I've known him for some years. Flavian was what threw me. We always called him Flav. As I recall, he retired a few years ago from the Bureau."

"Do you keep in touch with him?"

"No, not really. I got one card from him when he

was in Chicago some months ago. He gave no return address."

"You haven't seen him or talked to him in how long?"

"Not since he retired about three years ago. I was at the small ceremony. He seemed unhappy about having to quit, but his eyes just wouldn't hold up to the daily engraving work. Too bad, he's a fine engraver."

"Is there any reason he might send you something for safekeeping?"

"No. We weren't good friends, just acquaintances."

The general placed the letter to him on the table. It had been trimmed and reglued where it had been opened.

"This letter came to you recently and we believe it is from Mr. Kirby. Would you be so kind as to open it for us."

"You violated my privacy and my U.S. mail privacy . . ."

"We had a search warrant, Mr. Whitmore. Please open the letter."

He tore open the envelope, anger showing in his eyes. "Why could you get a search warrant? I don't understand."

"Read the letter, and tell us about it," the general purred.

Whitmore read the letter and shook his head. "I can see nothing unusual and certainly not illegal with this note. How could you get a search warrant?"

"What else is in the letter? What does he want you to keep for him?"

"I don't know. Let's look."

He unwrapped the heavy paper from around the thin package and gasped when the plates for a $20 bill fell out.

"What in the world?" Whitmore looked at both men in shock and surprise.

"Oh, my God! I knew that we had a report that one of the old plates had been tampered with and that a front and back of the twenty had been cut off, but I had no idea . . ."

General Halleck stood and held out his hand.

"Mr. Whitmore, we apologize for putting you though this minor ordeal, but it was important to us to know if you were working with Flavian Kirby on this counterfeiting. We have him in custody. He's the one who stole the plates. He also printed up $88,000 worth of the bills, but all had the same serial number. We recovered most of the fake bills. Now we have the plates and the case is wrapped up."

Whitmore stood and shook his head. "Kirby. I knew he wasn't happy about having to retire, but I never thought he'd go this far. The bills must have been terribly hard to detect. I swear, I never would have guessed that about Kirby."

They shook hands all around and Whitmore was taken by cab to his home where he said he needed to check some things before he went back to the mountains to finish his vacation.

When Whitmore was gone, the General shook McCoy's hand.

"Well done, as usual, McCoy. Now tell me, working with Agent Flanders wasn't really so difficult after all, was it?"

"No sir. She more than pulled her weight on both cases."

"Good. The next time I feel an expert could help you in solving a case, I hope you don't have a nervous fit when I send one along, male or female. Now, as far as I'm concerned, you're free to head back to St. Louis in the morning. I'll be in touch with you about a pair of new cases in your area that we're putting together right now. Take off a day or two and at least catch up on your laundry."

McCoy grinned, went out of the office and along the hall to the stairs. Jessica was waiting for him there. She linked her arm through his, and they went down the steps.

"I hear you're to go back to St. Louis tomorrow," she said.

"Yep."

"So that means we have until the eight o'clock train in the morning, right?"

"Yep."

"Any ideas?"

"Yep." He chuckled. "Now that you mention it, I'm in the mood for a good big steak dinner and then some soft and tender ministrations through the evening and far into the night."

Jessica pressed his arm tightly against her breast. She looked up at him, her eyes brimming with desire.

"I think we better go to my apartment rather than some stuffy old hotel room. I've got just all sorts of plans for you until the wee hours of the morning."

McCoy laughed softly and kissed her cheek. Already

he was thinking about the long night that stretched ahead of them.

"Oh, yes, Jessica," he said, and they hurried down the street.